BOUND BY FRIENDSHIP

A COZY QUILTS CLUB MYSTERY

BOOK 8

MARSHA DEFILIPPO

FREE BONUS MATERIAL

The case is closed... but the spirits aren't resting.

In this exclusive bonus story, the Cozy Quilts Club uncovers a lingering secret that the police missed. From Sarah's high-tech ghost-hunting to Eva's sharp-witted Maine Coon cat, see what happens the moment the yellow tape comes down.

Claim your free copy in Ebook or
Free Audiobook

To get the latest information on new releases, excerpts and more, be sure to sign up for Marsha's newsletter.

CHAPTER 1

The aroma of cinnamon filled the kitchen. Eva Perkins hummed along with the radio while she bustled around the room preparing for a get-together with her friend, Maggie Larkin.

They'd set up the visit the week before when Maggie had called Eva out of the blue during the weekly meeting of the Cozy Quilts Club. Eva was one of the four women in the club, each of them possessing a paranormal ability which they'd used several times to solve murders in their little town of Glen Lake, Maine.

Eva's cat, Reuben, followed her movements from his perch near his bowl, now devoid of food, hoping to catch her attention. The tip of his tail twitched as his irritation grew when she continued to ignore him.

Ahem, he said at last. *You seem to have forgotten something.*

Eva looked up distractedly from the sink where she was washing dishes.

He looked pointedly down at his empty bowl and then back at Eva.

"Oh, right. I'm sorry, Reuben. I've been so busy, I completely forgot," Eva said, and dried her hands on her apron.

She hurried to the cupboard and found his favorite canned

food, then dolloped a generous portion into his dish. Reuben wasted no time devouring it. The sound of the doorbell interrupted his post-breakfast grooming.

"That must be Maggie." Butterflies fluttered in her stomach. Maggie hadn't explained the reason for wanting to see Eva, but she knew intuitively it wasn't just for a reunion.

Maggie? The Maggie who has a dog?

"Yes, Reuben. The Maggie who has a dog. But she's not bringing Ginger with her today, so you can relax."

Reuben gave her what he thought of as his withering look, trotted into the living room, and jumped onto the cushion in the bay window area. It was where he spent the majority of the day, napping in between surveying the world beyond his domain.

"Oh, it's so wonderful to see you again," Eva said, embracing her friend before stepping aside for her to enter.

"You too, Eva. You know how I get when I'm working on a story," Maggie said, handing her jacket to Eva. "Time slips away from me."

"Preaching to the choir. Although for me, it's when I'm putting together a new quilt project."

Eva took a closer look at her friend, an investigative reporter for Channel Eight, one of the local TV stations. She was an attractive woman in her mid-fifties, tall and slender. Her dark brown hair was cut in a stylish bob. Even in jeans and a pullover sweater with a button-down shirt underneath, she looked like a fashion model. But beneath the polished, put-together façade, Eva sensed a nervousness she'd never seen in her before.

"Oh, my gosh! What is that heavenly aroma?" Maggie asked.

"I made a batch of cinnamon rolls this morning. Would you rather have coffee or tea to go with yours?"

"Tea, please."

"Make yourself comfortable in the living room, and I'll be right back. You take it with a dash of milk, no sugar, right?"

"You've got a great memory," Maggie replied with a smile.

"Well, hello, Reuben. Aren't you looking handsome this

morning?" Maggie gushed when she spotted the feline sitting upright on his cushion, staring at her.

Typical human. I'm always handsome, he retorted, with a hint of derision. Unlike Eva, Maggie couldn't communicate with him, so his thoughts had no impact.

Eva entered the living room carrying a tray with cups, napkins, and two plates with a cinnamon roll on each. She responded to his comment with a glare, but didn't speak. Maggie didn't know about her gift of the ability to communicate with animals.

Reuben got the message and curled up on his cushion with his back to the women.

"I've been following your reports about Wayne Harrington. You really broke that story wide open. It's even been on the national news."

"It's the most difficult story I've ever done. And the only one that has ever received this much attention," Maggie replied.

"His trial is coming up soon, isn't it?"

"The end of the month. I've been working with the DA's office, and they'll be calling me as a witness."

Eva caught the tremble of Maggie's hand when she put her mug on the coffee table.

"This has you frightened, doesn't it?" Eva asked.

Maggie met Eva's eyes, and she saw the worry there. The air in the room became charged.

"I've never been more frightened. I've worked on stories about corruption before, but this one is different. Wayne Harrington is different. People who cross him end up missing or dead, but they've never had enough evidence to prove he's responsible. Despite his assets being frozen, he must have accounts hidden because, according to my sources, he still has money and resources that make him dangerous."

"Are you sure it's necessary for you to testify?"

"The DA's office seems to think so. Getting the truth out to the public is what I've built my career on as a journalist."

"What are they doing to protect you?" Eva leaned forward. Her body tensed, thinking about what could happen to her friend.

"They're going to put me in a safe house, but I can't take Ginger with me. I was hoping you would watch him while I'm gone."

"Of course! That would be no problem at all."

Behind Eva, Reuben growled low in his throat.

Eva was quiet for a moment. "You're brave, Maggie. I don't know if I could do what you're about to do."

Maggie relaxed. "You're a good friend, Eva. Having friends like you is what makes my bravery possible," she said, with gratitude in her eyes.

"When should I be ready?"

"I might have to call you at the last minute. They don't want to take any chances of a leak, so they haven't been very forthcoming with details." Maggie fished in her purse and pulled out an envelope and handed it to Eva. "This is a key to my house just in case I have to leave before you get there."

It felt heavier to Eva than its contents should have; weighed down with the responsibility she was accepting on behalf of her friend. Her fingers gripped the envelope, and a chill crept over her.

"You mentioned a new quilt project. Can you show me?" Maggie asked, shifting the conversation to a safer topic.

Eva knew Maggie was intentionally changing the subject and was grateful to move on.

"Yes! My quilt club picks a different quilt design every month, and we chose Friendship Star this time. We've become very close since we started the club, and I suggested we commemorate our friendship with a design created to celebrate it."

"What a lovely idea!"

"Follow me. I have a few blocks started."

Maggie's eyes rounded when she walked into Eva's craft studio.

"It's like I'm walking into a quilt shop," she exclaimed as she looked around the room.

Eva chuckled. "I don't think you've been here since I renovated part of the garage to turn it into my craft haven. I knew I'd need something to keep me busy after I retired, and this has been perfect."

"Look at all that fabric!" Maggie said, scanning her eyes over the wall of six-foot-tall bookcases filled with material and quilting supplies.

Eva's cheeks turned pink.

"I've been told it's not hoarding if you actually use what you save. I'd been buying and stashing fabric for years with the idea I'd have it on hand for retirement. It hasn't stopped me from buying more since, but I'm making an effort of seeing what I have on hand first."

This time Maggie chuckled.

"You don't have to justify this to me. I'm happy to see you have a purpose. Too many folks just sit in their recliners all day because they didn't develop hobbies earlier in life."

"That is definitely not me."

Eva walked to her cutting table with Maggie on her heels. Spread out on the table were stacks of assorted cotton material. Some were long strips, and others were squares. Six blocks were assembled and arranged in a row.

"I sew the long strips together, then cut them into triangles. These squares will be the center of the star. And the white squares form the borders for each nine-patch block." Eva pointed to the stacks as she explained the process.

"How do you make the strips into squares?" Maggie asked, her brow furrowed.

"Let me show you."

Eva took a strip that had already been stitched together on

the long sides of the strip and demonstrated the technique for Maggie.

"Here's where the magic happens," Eva said, grinning, and opened up the triangle to display a square of white on one side and the colored fabric on the other. "It's called a half-square triangle. There are a lot of ways to make them, but I had these pre-cut strips already and wanted to use them up."

Maggie picked up a finished block to study it, deconstructing it in her mind.

"I see it now. You have three rows across and down and turn the pieces you just made to a different angle. Then you fit them in between the white pieces with the square in the middle of the colored fabric, and that's what makes the star design."

"You've got it. I knew you'd be able to see it. Maybe you should join our quilt club," Eva said, pleased with how quickly Maggie grasped the concept.

"Maybe when *I* retire," Maggie said with a smile. "I don't think I could sit still long enough to make an entire quilt."

"If you ever change your mind, I'd be happy to teach you the tricks of the trade," Eva told her.

Maggie glanced at her watch.

"I should really get going. I need to make sure I have everything ready for you. Ginger is going to need her own go-bag," Maggie said, joking. "I'll print out instructions for her food schedule and the name and contact info for her vet, too."

They walked back to retrieve Maggie's jacket and stood for a moment locked in an embrace, each of them knowing the stakes for Maggie.

"Don't you worry. Ginger will be in good hands. Everything's going to be just fine," Eva told Maggie, releasing her from the embrace.

They both knew it was a promise she couldn't guarantee, but didn't want to bring their mood down even more.

"Thanks, Eva. I'll be in touch soon," Maggie said, waving

back at Eva before sliding into her car and backing out of the driveway.

Eva watched with a sense of unease as her friend drove away. Her fellow quilter, Annalise Jordan's warning the day before echoed in her mind—Maggie was in danger. Eva had chosen not to repeat it, afraid Maggie would dismiss a psychic's vision. But what if it were true? Eva closed the door, her brow furrowed with worry.

I should have found a way to tell her.

Those words would come back to haunt her later.

CHAPTER 2

The mug of coffee warmed Annalise Jordan's hands, and she held it closer to let the steam float up to her face. It wasn't cold in her sitting room. She knew that, but looking out the window at the field of white snowdrifts gave her that impression.

She set her cup down, closed her eyes and rested her head on the back of the wingback chair, letting her mind wander. The soft spa music from her CD player lulled her into an even deeper state of relaxation and then faded into the background.

Visions often came unbidden when she was in this state. It was part of being a psychic, and after more than fifty years, she'd accepted them without question or fear—mostly. Every so often, though, the visions were warnings of imminent danger. Today her body tensed with that anticipation of danger as, in her mind's eye, Annalise was transported to a home she didn't recognize.

But she did recognize the woman sitting at her kitchen table, sipping from a mug. Lying asleep beside her on the floor and snoring softly, Annalise saw an Irish setter, its head resting on its paws.

It's Maggie Larkin. The name popped into her head.

A doorbell rang, and Maggie looked up from the newspaper she was reading. Her brow creased with worry, and the dog jumped up to bark at the unseen visitor.

Who can that be? she asked, but only the dog was there to hear her.

The dog bounded out of the room toward the door, and Annalise's POV changed to follow the woman when she rose from her chair.

Hush, Ginger, she told the dog and pulled aside the curtain covering the front door's sidelight to peek at the visitor.

The movement of the curtain caught the attention of one of the two men standing outside, and he held up his badge and identification for Maggie.

"I'm Agent Malone, and my partner is Agent Fitzpatrick. We're here to take you to the safe house."

The other man held up his identification for Maggie to see. Satisfied, Maggie opened the door to let them in.

"I just need to get my bag. It's already packed, and I'll need to let my friend know she should come to pick up Ginger."

She turned to retrieve the bag from where it was sitting beside the stairway to the second floor. As soon as she did, a cloth was pressed to her face, and she struggled to free herself from the arm that held her tight. Annalise felt her panic as if it was her own, before Maggie lost consciousness.

Ginger barked furiously and jumped on the man holding Maggie's now limp body, digging at the man's arms to make him release her.

Get this dog off me, the man who'd identified himself as Malone shouted to his partner as he shook his arm to disengage Ginger.

Fitzpatrick grabbed Ginger's collar and pulled him off. The dog squirmed under his collar, twisting his body to get away.

Find the bathroom and stick him in there.

Fitzpatrick walked down the hallway, still holding onto the dog despite Ginger's attempts to struggle free. On the right, he located the bathroom and with his free hand grabbed the door handle, pulling the door toward him. When he judged it safe to do so, he released Ginger and slammed the door shut.

Malone had carried Maggie to their car and laid her down in the back seat. Fitzpatrick grabbed Maggie's suitcase, closed her front door, and tossed the suitcase in the trunk. Malone got into the passenger seat, and they backed out of the driveway onto the street.

Annalise jolted out of her dream state, her heart pounding in her chest. She grabbed her phone and pressed the button on her Favorites list. The moment the connection clicked, she blurted, "Eva, it's Annalise. Maggie's in trouble."

CHAPTER 3

"**A**re you sure they're gone?" Eva asked when Annalise finished.

"Yes, I'm certain."

"I'm going to call her, and if I don't get an answer, I'll go over to see if she's okay. It's not that I don't trust your vision, but maybe it hasn't happened yet. No offense."

"None taken, but, Eva, you shouldn't be there alone. Take Jim with you. I don't think I'm wrong about this."

Eva opened her mouth to object, but realized it was good advice. "I'll call him if Maggie doesn't answer."

"If you can't reach him, call me back and I'll meet you there."

"I will. I promise," she added, anticipating Annalise's next words.

Eva dialed Maggie's number, willing her to answer, but the call went to voicemail after four rings, her body tensing with each one. Accepting that Annalise could be right, she disconnected the call and dialed Jim's number.

Jim Davis, a retired state police officer and Eva's romantic partner, answered on the second ring.

"Good morning, sweetheart. To what do I owe this honor?" he asked, teasing.

"I need you with me…"

"I love being propositioned in the morning," he interrupted.

"Be quiet for a minute," Eva said, her response tinged with annoyance.

On the other end of the line, Jim's smile was replaced with concern, and he waited, as instructed, for Eva to continue.

She repeated Annalise's vision. "I'm going there now to check on her and Ginger, but Annalise thinks you should come with me."

"I'll pick you up in five."

Eva held the phone away to check the screen, unsure if he'd actually disconnected the call before she could reply.

Jim arrived in four minutes, and Eva, already in her coat and purse in hand, stepped out to join him. As they drove, Eva filled him in about Maggie's visit the day before.

"What if Wayne Harrington got to her first?" Eva asked, anxiety gnawing at her.

Jim glanced over and patted her hand to reassure her when he recognized the worry in her voice. "Let's see what the situation is first."

As soon as they arrived and Jim shut off the car's engine, they heard barking coming from inside.

"That's Ginger. Annalise must be right about Maggie. He sounds frantic."

"You wait here and I'll check to see if there's a way to get inside."

"I've got a key," Eva said, fishing it out of her purse and handing it to Jim.

Jim knocked first and then used the key when no one answered. He followed the sound of Ginger's barking and was nearly knocked over when he opened the door.

"Easy, boy, easy," Jim spoke in a soothing tone, but the dog continued snarling at him, with teeth bared and hackles raised.

Eva appeared in the hallway and called to Ginger. The dog

looked at Eva and then back at Jim, giving him one final bark of warning, and ran to Eva.

"It's all right, Ginger. Jim is a friend," Eva said, kneeling down to stroke Ginger's head and scratch under his chin. "Tell me what happened."

Ginger recounted the events leading up to his imprisonment in the bathroom. When he was finished, Eva translated for Jim.

"I'll call Deputy Tremblay," Jim said, taking out his cell phone.

Ginger growled low in his throat and shifted his focus to the front door. Eva and Jim followed his gaze just as the doorbell rang, which set off Ginger's barking again, and he lunged toward the door before Eva could stop him.

"Take Ginger and go back to the bathroom. Ask him to stay quiet while I see who it is," Jim told Eva.

"Follow me, Ginger. Jim will take care of this." The dog reluctantly turned to obey. "Be careful. Don't take any chances," she said to Jim, barely above a whisper as they passed him.

He gave her a quick kiss on the cheek and waited for them to return to the bathroom. The doorbell rang three times in quick succession and was immediately followed with a rapping on the door.

"Ms. Larkin, it's Agents Malone and Fitzpatrick."

Jim opened the door to find two men in suits standing on the porch, both with surprised expressions when they saw him.

"Who are you?"

"My name's Jim Davis. Can I see your identification before I let you in?"

The men presented their IDs for his inspection and, satisfied they were legitimate, Jim invited them in and closed the door behind them.

"I'm here with my partner, Eva Perkins. She's a friend of Maggie's." Before continuing, he called out to Eva, "It's safe to come out, Eva."

The bathroom door opened, and Eva walked to the group of

men gathered in the entryway, with Ginger following behind, calmer than when they'd first arrived, but still visibly nervous. Jim introduced them, and they took seats in the living room.

"Why are you here?" the man named Malone asked.

"Maggie asked me to watch her dog while she was away," Eva offered, but chose not to mention the safe house. "Why are *you* here?" Her nerves were still on edge despite knowing Jim wouldn't have allowed them to enter if he had doubted their credentials.

The men exchanged glances, and Fitzpatrick nodded his assent for Malone to continue.

"We were sent by the DA's office to take Ms. Larkin to a safe house during the trial for Wayne Harrington. Did she tell you why she was leaving and where she was going?"

"No, and I don't think she left voluntarily. She'd told me she would call first to let me know when I should pick up Ginger. She didn't do that, and I know she would never just leave Ginger locked up in the bathroom."

"What prompted you to come here if she didn't call?" Fitzpatrick asked.

Eva hesitated, knowing how it would sound if she told them her psychic friend had warned her Maggie was in danger or Ginger's account of Maggie being abducted. It wasn't the best explanation, but instead she said, "Woman's intuition. I had a feeling something was wrong."

The agents didn't push her for more, but one arched a skeptical brow and the other's lips pressed thin in doubt.

"What did you find when you arrived?" Fitzpatrick asked.

"We only got here about five minutes before you did," Jim replied. "We could hear the dog barking and went to let him out. We haven't looked around the rest of the house."

"Stay here then while we do that now," Malone told them.

"I'll go upstairs. You look around here," Fitzpatrick said to Malone.

The men returned in just a few minutes.

"It doesn't look like there are any signs of struggle," Malone reported and appeared to be more perturbed by that than if he had found any. "Are you sure Ms. Larkin wouldn't have just taken off? Maybe she got nervous about the trial and decided to leave town instead?"

"I'm sure. And I don't like the insinuating tone you're taking," Eva said, prickling. "Did it occur to you to look in the garage for her car?" Her anger rose to a low simmer as she defended her friend.

Jim rubbed his finger under his nose, covering his mouth with his palm to suppress a grin upon hearing Eva's feisty tone.

"It's in the garage, but that doesn't mean she didn't leave on her own. She could have called a cab or had another friend give her a ride," Fitzpatrick said, a tone of defensiveness in his voice.

"She would not have left Ginger locked in the bathroom. And she would have called me first to come get him, or more likely, she would have taken him with her," Eva replied tersely. An idea popped into her head, and she took her cell phone from her purse and found Maggie's number. They all turned toward the kitchen at the sound of a phone ringing. Eva looked at the men, a smug expression on her face. "And she wouldn't leave without taking her phone."

"Go check it out," Malone told Fitzpatrick.

"And while you're there, look for a bag with Ginger's name on it," Eva called to his retreating back.

The room was quiet, but they all felt the tension in the air.

Fitzpatrick reappeared a moment later holding the cell phone in one hand and a canvas bag in the other, looking sheepish. "It was underneath the newspaper. The bag was on the counter."

"Now will you believe me?"

The men sighed in unison, admitting defeat.

Malone took his phone from his inside jacket pocket and punched a number.

"It's Malone. We've got a problem. I'm at Maggie Larkin's house, and it looks like she might have been abducted."

CHAPTER 4

"I know you're scared and confused, Ginger, but it's going to be all right. We're going to find Maggie, and you'll be home with her soon." Eva hoped her voice sounded more confident than she felt, for Ginger's sake. "I'll bring you inside and introduce you to Reuben so you can get acquainted while I bring in your food and dog bed."

Inside, Reuben was approaching the front door to greet Eva, unaware she had a visitor with her.

"Speaking of the devil, there's Reuben now," Eva said cheerily when she opened the door.

Reuben stopped dead in his tracks, tail twitching, and his ears laid back.

What is that? he demanded.

"Reuben, this is Ginger. Ginger will be staying with us for a while. You remember Maggie Larkin, who visited the other day? This is her dog, and Maggie asked me to watch him while she was away. Ginger, this is Reuben."

You can't be serious. Exactly how long will that be?

Eva fought back the lump in her throat. Her emotions were still raw. "I don't know, Reuben. Maggie has been abducted. It all depends on how long it takes the authorities to find her."

And what if they don't?

"*Reuben*! Don't even think that! They'll find her, and she'll be home, and Ginger can go back to his own house."

Ginger's anxiety had risen as he watched the exchange. It was bad enough that Maggie had been taken by the strangers. Now, he'd have to stay in a place where he wasn't welcome? This was turning out to be the worst day of his life. He lay on the floor and rested his chin on his paws, his tail curled against his body.

Eva bent down to reassure him. "Don't mind him, Ginger. He can be a grouch sometimes, but as far as I'm concerned, you're welcome here." She placed her lips close to his ear and whispered, "Give him some time. He'll come around."

That's what you think. And yes, I heard you—I'm not deaf. I'll be in your bedroom. Close the door after me. I don't want that beast anywhere near me. Reuben turned on his heel and stomped—as much as a cat can do so—off to Eva's bedroom.

Eva's heart squeezed when Ginger looked up at her, his eyes sad and he whimpered softly. She stroked his head gently.

"I'll be right back in with your things, and we'll get you comfortable. You're safe with me."

CHAPTER 5

Eva tidied up the kitchen with Ginger lying on his dog bed in the corner. Her mind was occupied with different scenarios of where Maggie could be and whether she was safe playing on a loop. She hadn't slept well the night before after discovering Maggie had been taken, and the lack of sleep was taking its toll. She jumped, brought back to the present, when the doorbell rang.

Jennifer Ryder was the first member of the Cozy Quilts Club to arrive for their meeting, but Annalise Jordan was right behind her.

"Where's Reuben?" Jennifer Ryder asked when they were back in Eva's kitchen. "And who's this?"

Ginger trotted over and sniffed Jennifer's hand.

"That's Ginger, Maggie Larkin's dog. Reuben is in my bedroom. He's been hiding out there and sulking since yesterday when I brought Ginger home with me. The poor guy's been beside himself," she said, stroking his head when he trotted back to her after deciding Jennifer was trustworthy.

"Have you had any updates about Maggie's whereabouts?" Annalise asked.

"Not since I called to let you know your vision was true,"

Eva said. Her face was lined with worry, shadows deepening beneath her eyes. "I need some advice about how to tell the authorities what Ginger told me."

Before Annalise or Jennifer could reply, the doorbell rang.

"That must be Sarah," Eva said. Ginger followed her to the door, unwilling to let Eva out of her sight.

"Well, hello," Sarah said, kneeling down to Ginger's level when she stepped inside. "Are you dog-sitting?" she asked, looking up at Eva.

"I am." Eva explained the circumstances on their way to the dining room to join Jennifer and Annalise. "Just before you got here, I was saying I need some ideas for how to fill in the authorities—but let's get dinner first."

The weekly meeting always began with a potluck dinner, often with a theme, that gave the ladies an opportunity to socialize before working on their quilt projects. Since it was February, this month's theme revolved around Valentine's Day. Heart-shaped pans and pink-tinted desserts covered the table in cheerful contrast to the heaviness of their conversation.

"If he didn't know about our potlucks, I think David might be getting concerned about all the 'love food' I've been making lately—especially when I leave with it," Jennifer joked, referring to her husband.

"Liam has been happy about it," Annalise said with a grin. "He's the lucky recipient of all my recipe tests. Since we've only been dating a couple of months, I'm relieved he hasn't thought I've been putting pressure on him about our relationship."

"Jim is just happy I've been cooking and sharing the meals with him," Eva said, chuckling.

"Same with Ashley," Sarah agreed. "She's had to travel a lot for work this month, so she appreciates my taking over the cooking duties. I think Max's been happy, too—he's getting more treats than usual."

"He might not be so happy if his vet puts him on a diet," Annalise cautioned, but her tone was playful.

Laughter rippled around the table, and then Eva's expression turned serious again. "Getting back to my dilemma, does anyone have any thoughts about how to do this?" Eva asked.

The mood in the room shifted as the others joined in her quiet concern.

After a moment, Jennifer spoke. "What about Maggie's neighbors? One of them might have seen something."

"Of course! That's so typical of me to overthink something," Eva replied, chagrined.

"In which case, the real agents probably questioned them already," Sarah offered. "Assuming they aren't worried about tipping the neighbors off that Maggie's missing."

"That's a good point, Sarah," Annalise said thoughtfully. "They might not want it getting out that the prosecutor's star witness has disappeared. Although now that I say that, the people who would *want* that to happen are the ones most likely responsible—so they'd already know."

"That's true, but you know how it is in small towns. Rumors spread like wildfires," Jennifer added.

"It's possible her absence won't even be noticed," Eva said, frowning. "Maggie would go away when she was following a story, so they might be used to it. Although this time is different. She might be away longer than usual, which is why she asked me to take care of Ginger instead of boarding him."

"We could ask her neighbor, Gloria Banks. She's a bit of a busybody, and I wouldn't put it past her to have been snooping out her window." Annalise pressed her lips together and frowned in derision.

Eva thought for a moment. "That's actually not a bad idea. I could pretend to be taking something to Maggie and knock on Gloria's door when Maggie doesn't answer. No—wait. That's not going to work either. She probably would have been watching when Jim and I were there. How about you, Jen? Could you go instead?"

"I could probably come up with some excuse. Maybe I could

take one of the dishes I've been trying out," Jennifer said, brightening when the idea came to her.

"That's a great idea!" Eva complimented.

Ginger gave out a small woof, drawing Eva's attention toward Reuben—who sat beside his food bowl glaring at the dog.

When is this beast *going to be gone?* he demanded.

"I've already explained this to you, Reuben. Until Maggie is found and the trial is over, Ginger will be our guest."

Your *guest. There's no* our *about this.* He narrowed his eyes at Ginger, who wisely kept his distance.

"Either way, you might as well accept the situation and try to make the best of it. You might even enjoy the company if you'd give Ginger a chance," Eva suggested.

Reuben's tail flicked. *Have you lost your mind, woman?* he asked, his eyes wide with disbelief. He gave her one last look of contempt before turning on his heels and trotting back to the safety of her bedroom.

"No need to translate," Sarah said with a grin. "I got the gist from your side of the conversation."

Ginger licked Eva's hand and whined softly. *Thanks for trying.*

"Of course, Ginger. Reuben is a curmudgeon, but underneath it, he has a soft heart."

I heard that! Reuben called out from the bedroom. *There's no need to insult me by suggesting I've got a soft heart. I'm a curmudgeon —through and through—and proud of it!*

Eva and Ginger exchanged glances. Eva shrugged her shoulders, and Ginger licked her hand once more, then lay down beside her with his chin resting on his paws.

"What do you say we move on to our quilting?" Eva asked.

"Works for me," Annalise replied.

"Me too," Jennifer and Sarah said in unison.

CHAPTER 6

Butterflies danced in Jennifer's stomach as she approached Maggie Larkin's door with a casserole carrier—even though she knew no one would be home. She rang the doorbell, and the hairs on the back of her neck tingled. She knew Gloria was watching but waited to the count of three Mississippis before returning to her car.

Jennifer put the dish on her car's passenger seat and looked across the street. The curtains in Gloria's window fluttered, and Jennifer suppressed a smile. She put on a show of pretending to change her mind, then retrieved the casserole carrier, closed the car door, and crossed the road to Gloria's house. It took only one round of knocks before Gloria opened her front door.

"Jennifer Ryder! What a surprise to see you," Gloria began innocently. "Come in, come in," she said, gesturing toward her living room.

I'll bet, Jennifer thought sarcastically, but held her tongue and accepted Gloria's invitation. *Whoa. The nineties called—they'd like their living room back,* she thought, stepping inside Gloria's home for the first time. The décor favored shades of mauve and teal, and beneath the crown molding, the walls were bordered with a floral wallpaper.

"Hi, Gloria. Actually, I was hoping to see Maggie Larkin. I made a batch of her favorite cookies, but no one answered the doorbell."

Jennifer held her breath, hoping Gloria didn't know what Maggie's favorite cookies were—since she'd made that up.

"Maggie isn't home, and something is going on over there," Gloria said, settling into the chair opposite Jennifer.

"*Really?* What do you think is going on?" Jennifer asked, leaning toward Gloria, playing into her bait.

Gloria's eyes lit up in anticipation of sharing some gossip. "Well, I saw a black sedan leaving Maggie's driveway the other day. I didn't recognize the men in the car, but they looked suspicious to me. And then a little later, Eva Perkins and Jim Davis showed up. Not long after that, *another* black sedan pulled into the driveway, and two more strange men—definitely not the same ones—got out.

Jennifer put on her best shocked expression. "My goodness, what do you think they were doing there?"

Gloria warmed to her story, thinking she had Jennifer hooked. "I don't have the faintest idea. But not long after they all went inside—I think Jim must have had a key because he walked right in—Eva and Jim came back out with Ginger and drove away. The other two men stayed there a few more minutes and then they drove off."

"But Maggie wasn't there?"

Gloria shook her head. "No, but later on I had this thought that maybe it has something to do with that Wayne Harrington trial. Maggie's supposed to be testifying against him, you know."

"So, you didn't see when the first car got there?" Jennifer asked.

"I was in the basement putting another load of clothes in the dryer and folding the ones I just took out, so I missed that," Gloria said with a trace of annoyance.

"But you saw the car when it left?" Jennifer pressed.

"Yes. Like I said, it was a black sedan. It didn't have any markings on it, but it looked like some sort of government car to me."

"Did you see the license plate?"

"It's like I told the agent when he called me later—"

"They talked to you about it?" Jennifer interrupted.

Gloria's chest puffed up as though she were the star witness in Maggie's disappearance. "Well, yes, just like on TV. His name was Agent Fitzpatrick. I told him the same thing I've told you already and that I could only see the first few numbers of the license plate. There was a two, a three, and an eight, but they drove away too fast for me to get the rest of it."

She sat back and folded her hands in her lap. "I hope Maggie is okay. I'll never forgive myself if something happened to her and I didn't see it."

Leave it to Gloria to make this about herself, Jennifer thought, but then she saw the genuine worry beneath Gloria's theatrics and felt a rush of sympathy for her. "But you only saw the two men in the car, so it's possible Maggie was already gone," Jennifer suggested, although she already knew it wasn't true.

"I hope you're right."

"Well, I should be going," Jennifer said, standing. "Thank you for filling me in."

"You're most welcome. I'll walk you to the door."

Jennifer was already on her way out when Gloria spoke again. "It's probably nothing, but I just remembered something. The driver of the first car tossed something out of the window as they were backing out of the driveway. I thought it was very rude to do that. Littering is a crime in this state." Gloria's lips were pursed in indignation.

"I'll go check it out now," Jennifer offered. "I keep a trash bag in my car that I can put it in if I find anything."

"I should have done that myself, but I got distracted when Eva and Jim and the other men came and then I forgot all about it."

Jennifer saw Gloria's look of genuine concern again. For all her nosiness, Gloria's heart was mostly in the right place, and her gossiping was the symptom of a lonely person trying to make connections. She knew she was still judging Gloria's behavior, but seeing that side of her softened it.

"It's no problem at all. I think I might leave a note for Maggie anyway, to let her know I was here. Thanks again!"

Jennifer waved and hurried across the street, where her car was still parked. After depositing the cookies in the passenger seat for the second time, she removed the trash bag she'd told Gloria about and scanned the ground near the driver's side. She felt her pulse quicken when she spotted a crumpled wrapper for a pack of cigarettes in the snow. *Maggie doesn't smoke. This has to be it!*

Her breath caught as the wind gusted and she thought it might blow away, but the snow must have melted during the day and then frozen it in place when the temperatures dropped again. She nudged the wrapper loose with her toe and used the bag instead of her fingers to scoop it up. All during her search, she'd sensed Gloria's eyes following her movements, so purposely looked over and held up the bag. "Got it. Just a cigarette wrapper," she smiled and called out, then tossed the bag in the car.

Jennifer forced herself to drive away at a normal pace, but once she was farther down the road, she stepped on the gas. She couldn't wait to get home to use her gift of psychometry on the wrapper. If she were lucky, she might get a clue about the driver.

"Hang on, Maggie. You've got people doing what they can to find you," she said aloud. She prayed they'd find her in time, but a chill ran up her arms at the thought of what might happen if they didn't.

CHAPTER 7

J ennifer had a couple of hours before her teenagers, Matt and Nicky, got home from school and several more before David would be back from the insurance agency they owned. Their dog, Boscoe, greeted her, tail wagging, as soon as she opened the door.

"Who's a good boy?" Jennifer cooed as she patted his head.

I am! Boscoe replied with a short woof. Without Eva to translate, Jennifer had to guess at the Jack Russell's meaning.

"I'm going downstairs," she told him as she put her coat in the closet. "You can come with me if you like, but I need to see if I can connect with what I've got in here." She picked up the bag with the wrapper, and Boscoe sniffed curiously.

I still can't believe I talk to a dog like this, she thought, *but since meeting Eva, I know he can understand me even if I can't understand him.*

Boscoe trotted after her to the basement rec room and curled up at her feet when Jennifer took a seat on the sectional. She slipped on a pair of nitrile gloves so she wouldn't transfer any of her own DNA onto the package.

A faint scent of tobacco wafted out of the bag when she reached inside. She held the wrapper in her upturned hands and closed her eyes. Visions didn't always happen when Jennifer touched an item, which was a good thing. She didn't want to live her life having a version of the Midas touch.

The room was silent, cocooned from the outside world. The windows were small, and curtains covered them this time of year to keep out any chilly February drafts. Jennifer hadn't bothered to turn on a light, hoping the dim light might provide the right atmosphere to focus her mind.

Jennifer prepped herself by taking several deep breaths and emptying her mind. She sat motionless for several minutes, but nothing happened, and she was afraid the gloves might have prevented making a connection. Sighing, she was about to toss the wrapper back in the bag, but when she grasped it tighter, her head jerked back and then an image flashed into her mind. She instantly knew she was looking through the eyes of a man. Ahead of him, with his back toward them, was a second man.

They were trudging through deep snow to a rustic cabin sitting in a small clearing. Pines, firs, and cedar trees towered above the cabin, and the bare branches of deciduous trees were mixed in among them.

"Get a fire going. I don't want to be freezing my butt off while I'm babysitting Larkin." The one from whose point of view Jennifer was seeing, told the other man. She felt the sting of freezing cold air as though it were her own cheeks exposed to the weather.

"How long will we have to be here?" He turned his head only slightly to reply so Jennifer couldn't see his face, but the vapor of his breath as he spoke floated up in the cold air.

"As long as it takes. Depends on whether Harrington decides he wants to keep her alive. I stocked the pantry with enough supplies for a week. If we need more, one of us can go back into town. It's not likely she'll be able to escape even with just one of us watching her."

Hearing his words sent another shiver down Jennifer's arms, but she concentrated on the details of the man ahead. She guessed he was probably six feet tall with a stocky build that wasn't just because of the puffy quilted jacket he wore. *No*, she corrected herself, *that's all muscle*, and a chill went up her spine as she thought of Maggie held captive by him. He was wearing a hat with earflaps that covered his hair and thick leather gloves. He had on snowshoes, and she looked down, seeing *her* man's feet in snowshoes, too.

Frustrated at not seeing more of his physical identifiers, she concentrated on the surroundings. The cedar siding of the cabin was stained brown, and it had a green metal roof. The chimney was located in its center, but there was no smoke coming out of it. It was sitting perpendicular to the direction they were approaching it from, and three steps led up to a small deck where she assumed the front door must be located.

If there was a lake or pond nearby, its surface was buried under the snow. The path ahead of them was unblemished by a human's touch. *No one's been here recently. We haven't had any new snow for at least a couple of weeks.* Jennifer heard the words in her head but at first wasn't sure if they were the man's or hers, before deciding they were her own. He'd already said he'd been there earlier to stock the pantry. She couldn't see any other structures nearby. Most cabins like this weren't heated and rarely used in the winter, but hardy sportsmen who liked to participate in winter recreation would brave the freezing conditions. Neighboring cabins might be hidden by the trees surrounding the clearing, but in her gut, Jennifer knew this location had been chosen for its isolation.

They'd reached the deck, and the man ahead had removed his snowshoes. Her heart beat excitedly as he turned to face *them*, and she realized she would be able to see his face.

CHAPTER 8

"Mom, we're home!" Matt called out, and the front door slammed shut, followed by Boscoe racing away to greet the new arrivals, barking as he ran.

The vision shattered, and Jennifer was back in her rec room. She shook her head to clear the disorientation she felt, and the room came rushing back into focus. "*Noo!*" she exclaimed in frustration. The wrapper was still warm in her hand. So close—she'd almost seen his face.

"I'm downstairs. I'll be up in a minute," Jennifer shouted back.

She scrolled to the voice memos app on her phone and closed her eyes. As she did, she played back the scene from her vision in her head and dictated it. She didn't want any of the details slipping from her mind when she shared them with the quilt club ladies. Satisfied that she'd captured it, she climbed the steps to join her teenagers.

"How was your day?" Jennifer asked. Matt and Nicky were at the kitchen table, a stack of cookies in front of each of them.

"Coach added more practices so we'll be ready for tourney," Matt replied through a mouthful of cookies.

"This will be your last year on the basketball team. Are you planning to try out at UMaine next year?" Jennifer asked.

"Yeah. I might not make the team, but it doesn't hurt to try."

"I like your attitude. How about you, Nicky?" she asked, turning to her daughter.

"Nothing special. Lots of homework, though. I think the teachers are piling it on to make up for our winter vacation coming up."

"Maybe that means they won't assign anything while you're on vacation."

Nicky rolled her eyes. "I wouldn't count on it. Especially not with Mr. Sanders. He *loooves* to give us homework during vacations. Somebody should point out to him the definition of vacation." She huffed out a breath in disgust. "Shouldn't he be retired by now?"

Jennifer hid a smile. She'd had the same complaint when she was in a class taught by Mr. Sanders nearly twenty-five years earlier.

"He's probably not as old as you think he is. He'd only been teaching a couple of years when I had him for U.S. History."

Nicky's jaw dropped. "He was teaching when *you* were in high school?"

Jennifer chuckled. "Yes, back at the end of the twentieth century." She pointed a finger at Matt when he opened his mouth. "And no comments about how old I am from the peanut gallery," she said sternly. He raised his hands, palms up, a wide grin stretching from ear to ear.

"Speaking of homework, we should probably start ours," he said to Nicky, and slid the strap of his backpack over his shoulder.

"Right behind you," she said, shoveling the last bite of cookie in her mouth.

"I had an interesting day," Jennifer began later that evening when Jennifer and David were alone.

"I'd love to hear about it." He was silent for a minute after she'd finished, then asked, "What do you plan to do about it?"

"I'm going to bring it up at the club meeting tomorrow and see what they think. For obvious reasons, I can't go to the police about it."

"You could take the cigarette wrapper to them. It must have some DNA on it," he suggested.

"But it hasn't been put out to the public that Maggie is missing. They'd want to know where I got the information."

"Good point. Maybe you could turn it over to Jim or Eva, and they could pass it along."

"Already thought of that," she said, smiling. "That's why I'm asking the boss if I could come in late for work tomorrow. I'd like to take it to Eva first thing."

"Good thing you have an understanding boss," he teased. "You have my permission to be late. We have a quiet morning according to the calendar."

"Thanks, hon. You're the best."

CHAPTER 9

"Have the kids left already?" Jennifer asked. "And good morning to you," she said, leaning down to pat Boscoe's head when he trotted over to her and licked her hand.

"Yeah, I told them not to wake you. Seems like you had a rough night," David replied.

"Sorry if I woke you."

"Only for a minute. From the looks of it, you weren't as lucky. But you're still beautiful," David said, grinning, and gave her a peck on the cheek.

"My vision followed me into my dreams. I didn't see anything new, but I'd wake myself up in a panic thinking about Maggie being kept in that cabin. And worrying that I should have turned over the cigarette wrapper as soon as I found it. What if they've already hurt her—or worse?"

Jennifer didn't need to explain. They both knew what "worse" meant.

"What's your gut telling you?"

Jennifer paused to take a mental body scan. "That she's okay. Scared—but okay."

"Then trust that. You'll hand it over to Eva this morning, and she'll make sure it gets to the agents in charge."

Jennifer nodded. "You're right. I'm a little better now in the daylight. Everything always seems worse in the dark in the middle of the night."

"Sorry, I can't stay longer, but I've got a call with a client scheduled this morning. Let me know how it goes. And don't worry about rushing into the office. Take as long as you need," David said, wrapping her in an embrace.

Jennifer rested her head on his chest, and her shoulders relaxed as the tension built up during the night loosened.

"Love you," David said, breaking the embrace, and picked up his briefcase before heading to the office.

"Love you, too."

Tires crunched on the snow as David drove away. Silence settled in, pressing against her as she sat with her mug of coffee. Her hand was shaking slightly from nerves as she reached for her phone and pressed Eva's number.

"Good morning, Jennifer!"

Jennifer let out her breath at the sound of another human voice. "Hi, Eva. Are you going to be home this morning? I have something I need to tell you and give to you. It's about Maggie."

"You must have talked to Maggie's nosy neighbor, Gloria Banks," Eva said, and Jennifer remembered Eva had probably been expecting a call about their discussion.

"I did, but I think I may have found a clue in Maggie's driveway. That's what I'm bringing. Would it be okay if I came over in about fifteen minutes?"

"Of course. I'll put on a fresh pot of coffee."

She disconnected the call and sensed Boscoe's eyes on her. "Sorry, Boscoe, I won't be back until dinnertime. You be a good boy while I'm gone."

I always am, he replied, but what Jennifer heard was *Woof!*

CHAPTER 10

ennifer arrived at Eva's house fifteen minutes later with the cigarette wrapper back in the bag. She told herself touching it wouldn't trigger another vision, but wasn't willing to risk it. One bad night's sleep was enough.

"Come on in," Eva said warmly when she opened the door. Her expression morphed into concern when she looked into Jennifer's eyes. "Oh, my goodness, you look like something the cat dragged in. No offense, dear."

And what exactly would a cat drag in? Reuben demanded, his tone huffy.

"It's just an expression, Reuben. But my guess is it would be something not in the best of health," Eva replied.

Jennifer smiled wanly. "No offense taken. I had a rough night."

"Let's go into the dining room and you can tell me all about it."

"I feel better already," Jennifer said, inhaling deeply the aroma of freshly baked blueberry muffins, the corners of her mouth lifting up with the hint of a smile.

Eva returned from the kitchen carrying two mugs of coffee

and slid one over to Jennifer. Ginger had followed close behind her and laid down with his body pressed against her leg.

"He's watching over you," Jennifer observed.

Reuben sat in the opening between the kitchen and dining room, keeping his distance from the dog. *He's* hovering. *It's unsettling.*

Eva gave him *the look.* "He misses Maggie—and he knows something's wrong," she told Jennifer, but the message was for Reuben, too.

"Is that what you brought me?" Eva asked, nodding to the bag that Jennifer had placed on the table.

"It is, but first let me tell you about my visit with Gloria and what happened after that."

Eva waited until Jennifer had finished her recitation before commenting. "I'm guessing you'd like me to turn this over to Agents Malone and Fitzpatrick?"

"Yes, for obvious reasons."

"Of course. I'll tell them I found it. I'm less worried about telling a white lie to a police officer than I am about finding the person this belongs to."

Jennifer was about to agree, then hesitated. "On second thought, maybe we should go together. If Gloria is watching the house, and they question her again, it would be better to have her corroborate that I was there."

Eva considered the suggestion, then shook her head. "No, that could raise too many questions. Especially about why I would have discussed Maggie's disappearance with you. I'll tell them I picked it up when Jim and I were there thinking it might be trash, but later I realized it could have been dropped by the kidnappers. That's why I waited to turn it over. And Gloria saw Jim and me there."

"That makes sense. I'll leave this with you, then. We should probably talk about all of this at tonight's meeting."

"Absolutely. I spoke with Annalise, but we need to bring Sarah up to speed."

Jennifer checked her watch. "I should go. I told David I'd be in this morning."

"Before you go, I'll wrap a couple of muffins to take with you," Eva offered.

Jennifer chuckled. "He might tell me to come in late every day if that became a habit."

"It works for all of us, then. I love to bake, but my scales aren't as happy about it if Jim isn't here to eat them, too." She took the plate with the muffins to the kitchen and returned with several in a paper bag for Jennifer.

"I'll tell you what the agents had to say when I see you tonight," Eva told Jennifer. "You look a little better than when you got here," she said, giving Jennifer an appraising once-over.

"Seeing you was just what I needed." She gave Eva a hug. "Thanks for the muffins."

Eva didn't close the door right away despite the frigid air outside. She waved when Jennifer looked up before backing out of the driveway. Only then did she return inside to find her purse and Agents Malone and Fitzpatrick's business cards that she'd tucked inside. Ginger nudged her leg, sensing her nerves. His warm weight against her shin grounded her.

Reuben lifted his head from his cushion where he'd been napping and blinked at her. *Oh, wonderful. The emotional support dog is reporting for duty.*

Eva shot him a warning look. "He's trying to help, Reuben."

Fine. Fine. Moral support noted.

Eva rubbed Ginger's head and murmured, "Ignore him. He's all bluster."

Ginger's tail thumped once in agreement.

"Wish me luck, Reuben. I'm about to fib to a police officer."

Make it good. I don't want to be put in a foster home if they lock you up. He yawned, stretched, and then put his head back on his paws to resume his nap, confident that was all he needed to say on the matter.

"Your concern for my welfare is touching," Eva said, her voice dripping with sarcasm.

Reuben opened his eyes but didn't lift his head. *You seem to forget—your welfare is my welfare, too. The two aren't mutually exclusive.*

"You've got a point," Eva said, recognizing the truth of his statement, but couldn't resist getting another jab in. "I'll do my best to lie convincingly."

Good woman. Now, can you just go make your call? I'm trying to sleep. As if to put an exclamation point on it, he got up, turned his back to her, and lay down again.

"Point, match." Eva muttered as she entered the phone number on the card. Her finger hovered over the "Call" button. Once she pressed it, there would be no going back.

This is for Maggie, she reminded herself, then pressed the icon to connect the call.

CHAPTER 11

The Club gathered around the kitchen island at Eva's, with the week's potluck supper dishes spread out buffet-style in the middle. In honor of February, all the dishes were a shade of red or pink from the pink beet hummus appetizer with red pepper slices for dipping, basil tomato soup starter, cheesy ziti and sausage with marinara sauce bake entrée, to the red velvet cupcakes for dessert.

"I just realized Ginger isn't here," Annalise said, looking around as though expecting to see him appear.

"He's having a sleepover at Jim's tonight. Reuben needed a break," Eva replied.

"He's still not ready to make friends?"

"That would be an understatement. He's finally venturing out of my bedroom for longer stretches of time. But he still hisses at Ginger whenever he gets too close for Reuben's comfort."

"It could be he just needs a little more time. He's been the king of this castle for years. He's not about to give up his territory without a fight," Annalise said.

"Hopefully, Maggie will be back soon so she and Ginger can be reunited. In the meantime, though, supper is calling to me," Eva said, ladling soup into a bowl.

"I think I just drooled on myself. This smells amazing," Sarah said, heaping her plate with some of each. "I'll be back for you," she directed at the cupcakes, eliciting chuckles from the others.

"Eva's already heard this, but I have news to share with the two of you," Jennifer announced once everyone was seated at the table with their selections. She summarized the events from her visit with Gloria to turning the wrapper over to Eva. "Now over to you, Eva. What happened with the agents when you gave them the cigarette wrapper?"

"I wish I could tell you they were excited to get it. But I think they wanted to dismiss it as trash someone threw out of their window and just happened to land in Maggie's driveway. There wasn't anything I could say to convince them otherwise." Her shoulders sagged, and her face reflected the sense of defeat the others picked up in her voice.

"Phil and Dennis wouldn't have treated you like that," Annalise said, defending her friend.

"Unfortunately, they're not the ones assigned to the case," Eva replied.

"They've helped us before," Sarah offered. "If they hadn't agreed to work with us to solve Lily Sullivan's murder, Meghan might be in jail right now."

Sarah's friend, Meghan Doherty, had been wrongly accused of murdering her roommate, Lily. The detective investigating the murder took the easy way of closing the case by accepting the circumstantial evidence at the crime scene instead of digging deeper. The Quilt Club ladies had reached out to their friends Phil Robertson and Dennis Smith, who were also homicide detectives they'd worked with on several cases. With their help, Meghan was exonerated.

"This case isn't a murder—at least we hope not," Eva said, her voice quavering. "It won't be as easy to involve them, but I'm open to suggestions."

The group was silent, each considering what, if anything, they could do to help.

Why don't you just ask them instead of assuming they wouldn't help? Reuben asked drily.

Eva jumped when she heard his voice coming from below her, where he was seated by her chair.

"You're absolutely right, Reuben. We should just ask. If they can't help personally, they'll tell us, but they might have some advice about what else we could do. Thank you!"

Reuben lifted his front paw to lick, pretending to be nonplussed by her gratitude, but they'd been together long enough for Eva to know he appreciated the thanks.

"In the meantime, I could start digging into Wayne Harrington's businesses. There might be some connections to associates willing to do his dirty work," Sarah offered.

"That's a great idea, Sarah," Jennifer complimented.

"Thank you. All of you," Eva said, glancing around at the others. "I don't think I could get through this if I didn't have your support... and your friendship. We couldn't have picked a better theme for this month's quilt."

"It's what friends do," Annalise said, smiling. "We've each been there for the other whenever we needed help."

I'm out of here before I have to cough up a hairball from all this touchy-feely stuff, Reuben said, and trotted back to the living room.

"That's you, Reuben. Sentimental to the end," Eva called after him, smirking.

No need to insult me, he replied without breaking stride.

"Anyone for coffee or tea to go with dessert?" Eva asked. "I thought I'd share some interesting facts I discovered about the history of friendship quilts before we go to our sewing stations."

"Tea for me, but I'll help get the table cleared while you're doing that," Jennifer offered and gathered up the now empty plates.

Several minutes later, Eva and Jennifer returned from the kitchen with mugs filled with the choice of beverage for each and the dish with the cupcakes.

Sarah didn't waste any time unwrapping a cupcake and biting half of it into her mouth. She let out a blissful sigh. "Mmm. These are delicious, Annalise."

"Thanks! I made them with you in mind." Annalise smiled at the praise. "You were saying something about the history of friendship quilts, Eva."

"Right. I found an article attributed to the Smithsonian that said friendship quilts began in 1855 in Northfield, Massachusetts. Charles Ripley was moving his family from there to Wisconsin. The friendship quilt was made by friends and family for his wife, Lucy, and given to her before the move. These types of quilts then became popular in the mid-nineteenth century when families relocated during the western migrations."

"They started right here in New England!" Jennifer commented.

"Yes. But here's the part that touched me. The quilts were assembled from blocks made by the friends and family and were accompanied by an inscription of the maker. They were meant to be a reminder of those the recipient left behind. I couldn't help thinking of Maggie."

Eva paused as her emotions took over. Annalise reached over to pat her hand to comfort her. Eva met her eyes, and a silent thank you passed between them. She cleared her throat and was able to speak again.

"I'd like to give my quilt to Maggie when she comes back, and I wondered if each of you would be willing to donate a block that I could include so she'll know we were all thinking of her. And we never gave up on her."

Her eyes glistened as she glanced around the table.

"Of course. I'd be honored," Annalise answered, her voice soft.

"Me too," Jennifer said.

"Me three," Sarah added.

Eva smiled, her heart full. "Then it's settled. I'll reach out to Phil or Dennis tomorrow. Sarah, follow up with digging into

Wayne's businesses—but be careful. You always are," she said, a smile tugging at the corners of her mouth.

Outside, the wind picked up, rattling the windows.

The hair on Annalise's arms raised. "Something's coming," she whispered.

The four women exchanged glances, each experiencing a chill that had nothing to do with the February air.

CHAPTER 12

Sunlight streamed in through the windows giving the illusion of warmth, but the thermometer mounted on the exterior of Annalise's kitchen window frame read ten degrees Fahrenheit. She shivered as she stared at the frozen landscape—but it wasn't the ten-degree chill outside that gripped her. It was the memory of last night's premonition.

The tea kettle whistled bringing her back to the present. She poured steaming water over the tea infuser she'd already filled with Earl Grey tea. The scent of bergamot filled her nostrils and her shoulders relaxed, but she couldn't shake the feeling that she was missing an important clue that would help Maggie.

"Stop trying so hard," she cautioned. "Just let it come to you instead of trying to force it."

Heeding her own advice, Annalise let it go and went about preparing her breakfast. The client for her first Reiki session wouldn't arrive for an hour giving her time for a leisurely meal. Perhaps even a short meditation to set her mental and emotional tone for the day.

She ate her meal mindfully, aware of every bite's taste, fragrance, and expressed gratitude for the opportunity to experience it. It kept her grounded and focused and by the end of the meal, her mind was clear. More at peace, she cleaned the kitchen and went to her Reiki studio—the former parlor of her 1800s era home to prepare for her client.

As she studied her client notes from their previous session, the words blurred. The room seemed to fall away, and she was seeing another place.

An oil painting of a pastoral landscape in a carved wooden frame hung on a wall. It slowly pivoted on hidden hinges to reveal a wall safe. A woman's finger pressed the numbers 5210 on the digital keypad on the door of the safe. The door opened. Sitting on top of several file folders was a flash drive. Annalise heard Maggie's voice: *Take this to Eva. She'll know what to do.*

Annalise blinked, heart pounding as the vision faded. Maggie's voice lingered in her head like a whisper through the ether: *Take this to Eva.*

The doorbell rang, pulling her back. On the other side of town, Eva hit "Send" on her message to Phil Robertson.

CHAPTER 13

"That was quick," Eva thought when her text notification dinged before she even had a chance to put down her phone. When she looked at the screen, though, it wasn't Phil returning her message. It was Annalise. The message was barely a sentence, but Eva's stomach tightened. Annalise didn't send cryptic instructions unless she was sure. 'Check behind the landscape painting in the carved wooden frame at Maggie's house. 5210 is the code. Can't say more now—have a client arriving for a session.'

Eva knew exactly which painting Annalise was talking about. She'd been drawn to its beauty whenever she'd visited Maggie and had even inspected it up close, but never had she suspected it might be hiding a wall safe.

"Well done, Maggie!"

Ginger tilted his head at the sound of Maggie's name and whined softly, catching Eva's attention.

"How would you like to take a ride, Ginger? We need to go to your house."

Is Maggie home now? he asked, his tail wagging enthusiastically.

"I'm sorry. Not yet," Eva replied, hating to disappoint him. It might have been a bad idea to suggest the ride, but she wasn't eager to leave Reuben and Ginger alone together. Reuben was already in a bad enough mood about sharing his territory.

That wasn't the only reason, though. *I don't want to be in Maggie's house by myself,* she admitted. *Plus, it won't raise any suspicions from Gloria if she sees me there with Ginger.* In the back of her mind, was the thought it was possible the men who'd kidnapped Maggie might come back. That put to rest any guilt she felt about rationalizing having him with her.

She grabbed her purse, making sure Maggie's spare key was there, her coat and Ginger's leash.

"We'll be back soon, Reuben. Behave yourself while we're gone."

Hearing the commotion, he'd ventured downstairs to see what was afoot.

Are you taking the beast back where he belongs? he asked, his expression hopeful.

"Not yet. Maggie's still missing but we need to look for something there. Annalise had a vision."

Reuben did his closest approximation of an eyeroll, but wisely held his tongue when he saw Eva's look of disapproval.

"We shouldn't be long. Enjoy having the house to yourself for a while. Come on, Ginger." She left without waiting for a response from Reuben.

As she was backing out of the driveway, her dashboard display announced an incoming call from Phil Robertson. She tapped on Accept and put the car in Park.

"I got your text. This is about the Maggie Larkin case?" Phil asked after they'd exchanged pleasantries.

"Yes. I know this isn't a homicide case, but Maggie is a friend and we have information that could help."

"Let me guess. It's not something you can tell the people in charge because they'd think you're crazy."

Eva chuckled. "You know us so well."

"And I know you're not crazy. What have you got?"

"Jennifer had a vision and Annalise may be onto something. I'm checking on it now. They both think Maggie is still alive and being held against her will. It's nothing solid yet, but we don't want to waste time explaining it. Would you and Dennis be able to meet with us at my house—maybe tonight around seven or seven thirty? We know you might not be in a position to get personally involved, but we'd appreciate any advice you can give us."

"I'll check with him and get back to you."

"Thanks, Phil. We owe you one."

"I'll put it on your tab," he teased and disconnected the call.

Eva's stomach clenched as she approached Maggie's house and parked in the driveway. She checked for fresh tire treads or footsteps in the snow, but nothing looked disturbed since her last visit.

Her fingers fumbled as she inserted the key in the lock, whether from the frigid temps or nerves, she wasn't sure. Ginger pushed ahead of her, his nose raised sniffing at the air. The house was eerily silent, the type of quiet that feels *too* empty. Without hesitation, Ginger walked to the living room and stood in front of the painting, whined softly, and then looked back at Eva.

I know I didn't say anything about the painting. I only read the text to myself, Eva thought, bemused, but followed the dog's lead.

She attempted to raise the painting up, thinking it was hung on the wall in the usual way, but it wouldn't budge. *Now what?* she thought. She stared at the painting, willing it to reveal how to make it move to get to the safe. An epiphany struck, and she pushed the frame in several spots before finding the spot for the pressure latch. She felt the slight push against her fingers as it released and let go as the painting swung open. Built into the wall was the safe with a digital keypad.

Eva took her phone from her purse to read Annalise's text again. She pressed 5210, heard the click of the lock, and the door opened just enough for her to take hold and open it the rest of the way.

Inside was a pile of file folders and on top, a flash drive. Eva removed it from the safe and as she stared at in her hand, for one wild second, she thought she heard Maggie's voice whisper, *Take it to Sarah.*

"Don't worry, Maggie. I've got it," she said, unaware she'd spoken aloud.

She put the drive in her purse and closed the safe, then pushed the painting against it, engaging the lock. The phone was still in her left hand and she scrolled to her Favorites list to call Sarah.

"Sarah, are you home? I found something at Maggie's I need you to see."

A car door slammed outside. Eva whirled in the direction of the sound, then froze.

CHAPTER 14

Ginger ran to the front door, barking all the way.

"Hold on just a minute, Sarah. I think someone's here."

Eva cautiously crept to the door, her nerves on edge. She slipped a finger under the curtain covering the sidelight beside the door and peeked outside.

"It's all right, Ginger," she said, letting out her breath. "It's just Gloria." She gave the dog a reassuring pat on his head.

"Eva? Are you all right? Eva?" Sarah's panicked voice coming from the phone in her hand finally penetrated her consciousness.

"I'm okay. False alarm. It was Gloria from across the street coming home. I'm at Maggie's house. I'll explain when I get there if it's okay to come now."

"Absolutely. I'll see you in a few."

Eva swept her eyes around the room, unsure what she was looking for, but other than the eerie silence she'd experienced earlier, nothing else raised any alarms.

"Let's go, Ginger. I'll introduce you to Max when we get to Sarah's. He's a lot more likely to give you a warmer reception than Reuben did."

Who's Max?

"He's Sarah's golden retriever."

Eva pulled the door behind them and locked it. Ginger's tail wagged as he pulled on his leash, eager to get to the car and meet a new friend.

———

The two dogs sniffed noses as Eva introduced them and she relaxed when they bounded up the stairs to Sarah's office.

"Looks like they'll get along just fine," Sarah said. "Do you have time for coffee? We can take it up to my office so you can tell me what you've found."

A few minutes later, they were in Sarah's sun-drenched second floor office, coffee cups steaming beside them as Max and Ginger played tug-of-war with Max's rope toy.

A smile tugged at the corners of Eva's mouth as she watched Ginger. "Thanks for letting me bring him. Reuben hasn't been the most hospitable host."

Sarah grinned. "Why does that not surprise me? So, what have you got for me?"

Eva removed the flash drive from her purse and handed it to Sarah, telling her about Annalise's text instructing her to retrieve it from Maggie's house.

"Let's see what we've got here," Sarah said, inserting the drive into the USB port on her computer. "It's password protected, but I have a program I can run. Maybe we'll get lucky."

"It's just a hunch, but try Woodstock1969," Eva suggested.

Sarah gave Eva an appraising look, but didn't question her before typing it in. "It worked!" she said, her surprise evident. "What made you think of that?"

Eva smiled, a coy expression on her face. "That's a story for another time. What's on the drive?"

"Several folders that don't appear to raise any red flags, but they could be decoys hiding the real information Maggie stored here." She opened files, clicking through them one after the other. "Whoa. This looks promising."

The file was labeled City Hall. Inside were documents linking Wayne Harrington to suspicious transactions and an MP3 file. Sarah clicked on it and they heard Maggie's voice: "Tell Eva if I disappear before I can turn this over, the answer's in the bank records."

A chill ran up the spine of both women as they held each other's eyes.

Eva's pulse thudded in her ears. "Do you see anything about bank records?" she asked at last.

"Not yet, but why don't you leave this with me and I'll go through the rest of the files?"

Eva's phone rang, startling them both. She answered, "Hi, Phil. I have you on speaker. I'm here with Sarah. We may have found something."

"Really? Well, it's good that Dennis can make it tonight. Still on for seven at your house?"

Sarah nodded in response to Eva's unspoken question.

"Yes. I'll get in touch with Jennifer and Annalise, but if they can't come, we can fill you in. See you then."

"It may take me a while to go through all the files and you probably don't want to sit here while I do that. I'll make a copy of this for them and bring it with me tonight," Sarah suggested.

"Sounds like a plan. Sorry, Ginger, but we need to go home now."

Do we have to? He looked up at her with puppy-dog eyes.

Sarah laughed. "Even I know what that meant. Why don't you let him stay and I'll bring him with me tonight?"

Both dogs' tails wagged and Eva could swear they were smiling.

"How can I refuse?"

CHAPTER 15

What *is* he *doing here again?* Reuben demanded that evening, his eyes narrowed from his perch in the bay window as he spotted Sarah leading Ginger toward the door.

"You were sleeping earlier and then I forgot about it or I would have told you that Ginger had a play date with Max today. That's why he wasn't here earlier. And he'll be here as long as it takes to find Maggie and bring her home."

Reuben kept any further comments to himself when Eva gave him a look that said she didn't want any sass from him on the topic of Ginger.

"And I'm having a special meeting of the quilts club tonight along with Phil Robertson and Dennis Smith. You can either mind your manners or find someplace to hide until they're gone."

I don't hide. *I remove myself from an unbearable situation,* Reuben replied, sitting up straighter and giving her his best haughty expression. *I'll be upstairs until this is all over,* he added before jumping down from the window seat and trotting up the stairs.

Ginger was the first to greet Eva when she opened the door. *I*

had such a good time with Max! Thanks for letting me stay. Can I go
back again sometime?

"That's up to Sarah," she replied. "Ginger wants to know if he can have another play date with Max."

Sarah secured the shoulder strap of her laptop bag in one hand and leaned her face to Ginger's level. "You can come anytime, Ginger. Max and I would love that!"

Ginger licked Sarah's face before she could stop him and then trotted to the kitchen to find his bowl of kibble.

"Should I set up in the dining room? It would make it easier to show everyone what I've found," Sarah asked.

"Of course. There's an outlet on the window side that would be close if you need to plug it in."

"Perfect. I'll go do that now. I think I hear another car driving in."

Fat snowflakes drifted down lazily, signaling a storm about to freshen up what was already covering the ground when Eva opened the door for Jennifer and Annalise.

"I brought cookies," Jennifer said, holding up a metal tin. "For morale."

"Thanks, Jen. Morale may be just what we need." Eva gave Jennifer a hug.

Eva looked closely at Annalise. Her face was pale, and her smile was not as bright as usual, but her eyes were alert. Her hands were shaking slightly as she removed her coat. Eva considered asking if she was all right but Phil and Dennis were walking toward the door. It could wait until a better time.

"Sarah's in the dining room. You two get yourself settled in and we'll be right there."

"It's good to see you again, Phil. Dennis. I didn't realize we had snow in the forecast or I would have suggested another time," Eva said as she stood to the side to let the men enter. Eva kept her voice even—she needed their help too badly to reschedule.

. . .

"It's not supposed to get bad until later tonight. We should have plenty of time to do what's needed," Phil replied, stomping his boots on the welcome mat.

"And from what Phil's told me about the case, better to do this now than later," Dennis added.

"Sadly, that's the truth. Follow me; the others are in the dining room. There's fresh coffee and Jennifer brought cookies."

"You had me at coffee, but the cookies are even better," Phil said, a big grin on his face.

Warm greetings were exchanged before they settled down to business.

Sarah had her laptop open and turned it so the others could see the screen. "I looked through all the files on the flash drive Eva brought me." She hesitated, then looked at the others. "You all know what I'm talking about, right?"

"She told us about it when she called us about the meeting," Jennifer assured her.

"Dennis is up-to-speed, too," Phil replied.

"Thanks for the heads up, Annalise. If it weren't for your vision, we might never have found the information."

"Glad to help, Sarah," Annalise replied, but Eva noticed again that her smile didn't quite reach her eyes.

There's something off. I need to get her alone to find out what it is, Eva thought.

As if reading her mind, Annalise glanced over at Eva and half-smiled. She gave an imperceptible nod of her head as though in agreement that they would talk later.

Eva brought her attention back to Sarah, who had begun her presentation.

"Most of what's on here isn't relevant but I found a folder labeled City Hall, and that one's a goldmine." She turned the laptop to click open the folder and selected a document before turning it back around to show them the spreadsheet. "These transactions link back to Wayne Harrington. I had to dig to get to the connections because they were made from shell accounts under different names on the surface."

She paused to let the others study the file.

"Where do you think she got the information?" Dennis asked.

Sarah clicked to a second document. "She had a source at the Planning office at City Hall. This is the part Maggie was digging into. Harrington's deals were always on the shady side, but still legal. This time there's proof he'd been bribing a City Hall employee to fast-track the property purchases."

"Do you mean the riverfront lots?" Dennis asked.

"Exactly. They were supposed to be designated for historical preservation, but Harrington got them zoned as commercial rental property. He was planning to build a luxury high-rise apartment building."

"Why did Maggie get involved?" Phil asked.

"Someone inside the planning department anonymously tipped Maggie off that Harrington bribed zoning officials to get permits approved even before public hearings were held. After that, she dug deeper—that's when she found her inside source there."

"That's what this trial is about? He used bribes to rezone land that wasn't even supposed to be sold?" Eva asked.

"That's right," Sarah agreed.

"It's not just him that has a lot to lose," Jennifer commented. "Did she say who's taking the bribes?"

Sarah frowned and huffed out a breath. "I haven't been able to find a name yet. She might have been cautious about writing it down in case someone found the flash drive before she could turn over the information to the DA's office. There were some notes that had initials—R.F.—and referred to them as her 'inside source.' I tried looking up the staff list, but didn't find anyone with those initials who works in the planning or zoning departments. It's possible she used a code only she could decipher to protect them."

"From what I found out from my contact at the DA's office, the prosecution has a case but without Maggie's files and her source, it's not solid. If she'd had time to turn them over, it might've sealed it. Her disappearance has stalled everything, but the court will only delay so long and he could still get off scot-free," Dennis said.

"So, it's a dead end?" Annalise asked.

Sarah smiled. "For now. Give me some more time and I'll crack it. Has Supersleuth Sarah ever let you down?" Her use of the moniker she'd given herself months earlier lightened the somber mood.

"Did you find anything that points to Harrington as the person behind Maggie's abduction?" Phil asked.

"Not yet, but if it's there, I'll find it." There was no doubt in Sarah's response.

Dennis added quietly, "If R.F. really exists and Harrington finds out, that person's in danger, too."

The room fell silent, each of them realizing the full weight of what Maggie had uncovered.

"Was there anything else we should know about?" Phil asked.

"Well, I found this in the notes she kept for herself." She opened the MP3 file. Maggie's voice filled the room: *Tell Eva if I disappear before I can turn this over, the answer's in the bank records.*

The words hung in the air and Jennifer whispered, "Oh, Maggie." No one moved after that for a long moment.

"Did she mean *more* bank records? You've already found the transactions about the bribes," Annalise asked at last.

"I'm not sure. Those records are critical to the case, but I've just got the feeling that there's more—and I'm going to keep digging just in case."

"Be careful, Sarah. Harrington's got friends in high places," Phil warned.

"You know I will. I'm pretty good at not leaving any foot-prints behind," Sarah assured him with a smile.

"So, what do we do?" Jennifer asked. "We can't just sit here while Maggie's still missing."

Eva folded her hands on the table, thinking. "Sarah, you've already got your assignment to keep digging through the files. Focus on anything that's tied to the banks or that could lead us to the men responsible for abducting Maggie. Annalise—see if you can tap into anything more. Your vision about the flash drive really moved us forward." She paused, still thinking. "It's probably unlikely, but I can ask Ginger if he might have over-heard Maggie talking to her source."

She looked at Jennifer. "Would you be willing to take the flash drive to try your psychometry?"

"Do you mean now?" Jennifer asked.

"This one's a copy," Sarah interrupted. "I put the one from Maggie's in our safe at my house. I didn't want to risk losing the original in case we need to turn it over. If it was a copy, Harring-ton's attorney could say it wasn't submissible."

Eva's face registered surprise. "Oh, of course. I hadn't thought of that. Maybe you could go to Sarah's and do it there?" she asked Jennifer.

Jennifer nodded. "I'm willing to give it a try. Let's talk later to figure out a day and time," she addressed Sarah.

"I'll reach out quietly to someone at the D.A.'s office," Phil offered. "There might be some chatter about Harrington's deal-ings or associates that we could follow up on."

"We'll need to be discreet. We're homicide detectives so it might set up red flags if we're asking about a bribery case," Dennis reminded Phil.

"That's why I said we'd reach out quietly," Phil repeated, but his smile softened the words.

Eva straightened her shoulders and looked around the room. "Then it's settled. We have our assignments and we'll follow the trail—*carefully*."

Jennifer raised her mug. "To Maggie," she said softly. "And to the friendship that binds us together."

They joined Jennifer, raising their own mugs and clinking them gently.

Annalise shivered, but no one seemed to notice. She'd felt a sense of something being wrong all day and it was growing stronger. It was hanging at the edges of her intuition, not close enough to grasp, but she knew time was of the essence. They needed to find Maggie—soon.

CHAPTER 16

She hadn't been tied up, but the window was barred and the door was locked. There was no other way out unless they decided to release her.

What if they just leave me here? She pushed the thought down for the hundredth time. Her resilient spirit wouldn't allow it. *Thinking like that isn't going to get you out of this mess. There's a solution—there always is. You just haven't thought of it yet.*

Maggie crept to the door and pressed her ear against it. The aroma of wood burning in the cast-iron stove in the living room was stronger here. The men's voices were low, but she knew they were arguing. She recognized one of the voices as the man who'd identified himself as Fitzpatrick, but the other voice was new.

"We should just dump her back at her house," Fitzpatrick said.

"Orders are orders. The boss said to make sure she never talks."

Her eyes slipped closed as she concentrated, holding her breath as she did. If she was asked to identify him later, it was the only way without seeing his face. The man's voice was distinctive—a gravelly baritone.

Fitzpatrick hissed, "I'm not going down for murder. The deal was to kidnap her and bring her here until they dismissed the case."

"Do you really think Harrington is going to let her loose? She could still blab and they could arrest him on different charges."

"Yeah, that's possible. But he's got expensive lawyers. He's always found a way to squirm out before. This won't be different."

The other man didn't have a response.

Fitzpatrick continued his argument. "And bribery's a lot less time in jail than murder. Even if he isn't the one doing it, they could still get him for putting out the contract."

That's right, Fitzpatrick. Keep pressing with that, Maggie cheered him on silently from her room.

"Maybe," the other man agreed begrudgingly. "You've got enough food to last a few more days?"

"Yeah, we're good. She doesn't eat much."

"All right. I'm outta here. Make sure your phone's charged. I'll text before I come back," he told Fitzpatrick. "But if Harrington says she's toast, no more arguments."

There was silence and then a door slammed and Maggie crept back to the bed. The room wasn't cold, but she wrapped the comforter around her to take away the chill of the words and her possible fate. She had to hold on. Surely someone would be looking for her. Tears threatened as she thought of Ginger, but she blinked them back. She couldn't fall apart now. *Keep yourself together. This is* not *going to be the end of your story.*

CHAPTER 17

Sarah stepped into the warmth of her living room and hung her coat in the closet.

"How was the driving?" her wife, Ashley asked. She was snuggled up on the couch with a blanket, tea, and her laptop. Max had been curled up against her, but jumped down from the couch to greet Sarah, his front paws resting lightly on her thighs.

"Not too bad yet. It's still snowing but hasn't accumulated much. The plows haven't even had to come out."

Ashley studied Sarah's face. There was something more there than a drive home in a snowstorm. "Bad meeting?"

"Productive... but disturbing. Phil and Dennis were there. Jennifer is going to come by tomorrow if the roads are clear. She's going to see if she can pick up anything on Maggie's flash drive. I'd taken the copy I made," Sarah explained.

"I didn't realize Phil and Dennis were getting involved."

"They're not—directly—but they agreed to help like they did with Meghan." Sarah recapped the evening's meeting for Ashley.

"You're being careful, right?" Ashley asked, her brows furrowed with concern.

Max sensed the tension in the air and jumped up onto the couch between the women, looking from one to the other. Sarah reached out to stroke his head, and he plopped down beside her, resting his head on her thigh.

"Always," Sarah assured Ashley. "But I have to help. I'd much rather be doing that by digging into the case on my computer than interviewing a ghost."

Ashley nodded. "I get it... really, I do," she added when Sarah gave her a questioning look. "But that doesn't mean I won't worry."

"What are you working on?" Sarah nodded toward Ashley's laptop, redirecting the conversation.

"Nothing quite as interesting as you. Notes for my store visits." Ashley worked as a district manager for a national retail pharmacy which required in-person meetings with pharmacy managers at the various stores in her district. She closed her laptop. "But it can wait until tomorrow. Let's watch some TV instead."

"That works for me. Something light. I've had enough drama for one day."

The next morning the ground was covered in a fresh dusting of snow—less than two inches—making travel a non-issue.

"I'm off. Remember..."

"Be careful," Sarah finished the sentence, grinning. "See you tonight."

"Come on, Max. Time to work."

Max followed Sarah up the stairs to her office where she'd spread papers across the table set against the wall opposite her computer station. It held a mix of printouts of transaction spreadsheets embellished with yellow sticky notes, a City Hall staff list, and printouts of Maggie's notes from a folder labeled "anonymous tips."

"I'm missing something," she muttered.

Max looked up from his dog bed, then laid his head back down when he realized she was talking to herself.

Sarah picked up a spreadsheet to examine it again, then laid it back down when it offered no new clues. She repeated the process with the other paperwork with the same results.

"There has to be another file I overlooked," she muttered again. She put the copy of the flash drive into her computer and scanned through the list of documents and folders. Mixed among the obvious choices was a folder labeled Recipes.

"Why would Maggie have a folder of Recipes on this?" She'd dismissed the folder earlier but opened it now and found several documents containing recipes.

She sat up straighter when she found a recipe that had been scanned and written in the margin was a sloppily handwritten note that had no connection to gingerbread.

Harrington using outside consultant again. Dale Kitteridge handled last problem. Be careful who you talk to.
T.G.

That had to be the inside source—hidden in plain sight in the Recipes folder mixed in with dozens of scanned cards that looked exactly the same.

But something nagged at her. The initials were wrong.

She leaned back in her chair, staring at the keyboard as she worked it through in her mind. Then a flash of inspiration struck.

"You didn't change the letters, Maggie. You shifted them."

She grabbed the City Hall staff list, running her finger down the list until she came to the name, Tara Greene. "There you are!"

At the same time, Max jumped up and ran down the stairs just seconds before the doorbell rang.

"Right behind you, Max."

As soon as she was halfway down the stairs, she recognized Jennifer as the arrival. They'd arranged last night for her to come this morning if the weather allowed. Max pushed past her to greet Jennifer when Sarah opened the door.

"I'm glad you made it. I just found a clue," Sarah announced while Jennifer removed her coat and boots and made sure to give Max attention.

Jennifer looked up in surprise. "You did? On the flash drive?"

"Yes! Maggie had hidden it, but I still can't believe I didn't find it before. I had a nudge to check the folder labeled Recipes and there it was. Maybe Annalise's psychic powers are rubbing off on me. Would you like some coffee before we head upstairs?"

"I'm good—already caffeinated for the morning," Jennifer replied, smiling. "Let's see what you found. But first, I should see if I can pick up anything from the drive."

"I'm still using the copy. I'll get the original out of my safe."

Jennifer pulled a pair of nitrile gloves from her purse and took the drive from Sarah who was looking at her oddly as she did so.

"I don't want my fingerprints on the drive just in case Harrington's attorney tries to claim the drive isn't legit."

Sarah groaned. "Why didn't I think of that? Now mine are all over it."

"I'm probably overthinking this. Let's stay positive. We're going to find Maggie and she'll be able to give this information to the prosecutor herself."

"Right," Sarah replied with more confidence than she felt. "I'll give you a minute to tune in."

Jennifer let her eyes fall shut and stilled her thoughts. After a moment she opened her eyes. "I heard Maggie say the name Tara Greene, but I didn't pick up anything about someone with the initials R.F.

Sarah broke out in a wide smile. She showed Jennifer the note on the monitor display and followed up with the staff list. "There's a Tara Greene in the Planning Office. This is the only T.G., and my spidey sense is telling me this has to be the one who wrote the note. I think she's the inside source."

"But I thought you said Maggie's notes had R.F. as the source."

"I think she was purposely disguising Tara's identity. It came to me when I was looking at my keyboard. Maggie just shifted the letters over. If she wanted to disguise the real source, it seemed like the kind of swap she'd make."

Jennifer looked down at the keyboard. "You're right. That has to be it! Supersleuth Sarah does it again."

Sarah beamed at the praise, but teased. "As if there was any doubt."

"But who is Dale Kitteridge?" Jennifer asked.

"No idea—but Tara might."

"Should we try to contact her?" Jennifer asked.

"I think we have to. She's the only lead we have, and she seems to know more about Harrington than just his zoning permits."

Jennifer nodded. "Let's do it."

CHAPTER 18

Sarah located the number for the Planning Office and made the call, putting it on Speaker so Jennifer could listen in. "Yes, I'd like to speak with Tara Greene, please," she said when a young-sounding woman answered.

"Tara's not in today. She took a personal day off. Can I help you?"

"No, thanks. I'll try again later." Sarah disconnected the call and shook her head. "She really shouldn't be giving out personal information like that. I hope she's just young—or new."

"Should we try to find her at home? She might talk to us in person if we show up and are friendly. I picked up the vibe that she wants to help Maggie, but she is scared."

"We can try. Give me a sec—I'll need to trace her address." It only took a minute before Sarah announced, "Got it! Not exactly the best part of town."

"I'm coming with you. You shouldn't go by yourself."

Sarah was about to argue, but reconsidered. "You're right. And you've got a friendlier attitude than I do. I can come off a bit harsh sometimes. I've been told I have resting witch face." The corners of Sarah's lips turned up at the PG version she'd used of the phrase.

It took twenty minutes to reach Tara's house—a run-down ranch on the outskirts of Bangor. Sarah parked in the driveway behind an older model SUV.

"Someone just peeked out the living room window. I saw the curtains move aside and then back down again," Jennifer said.

"Hopefully, she's alone."

Sarah knocked, and the door opened only as far as the chain lock would allow. A middle-aged woman with mousey brown hair peered out and her blue eyes darted from side to side as she surveyed the street.

"Tara Greene?" Sarah asked.

"That's me. Who are you?"

"My name's Sarah Pascal and this is Jennifer Ryder. We're friends of Maggie Larkin."

The woman's eyes grew round—full of terror—and the door slammed in their faces. Jennifer and Sarah stared at each other with shocked expressions, but then it swung open again, this time wide enough for them to enter. Tara gave the street one more glance up and down before shutting the door.

"How did you find me?" she asked nervously after they'd taken seats in her living room. The décor was more shabby than chic. A blanket was crumpled at one end of the tattered couch, giving the impression she'd slept there—and not well. The bags under her haunted eyes added to the appearance of someone who was teetering on the brink of a nervous breakdown. A half-full mug of cold coffee and a glass of water sat on the table between the couch and chairs where Jennifer and Sarah sat.

"We have a flash drive with Maggie's notes that she wanted us to have in case anything happened to her," Sarah said. Jennifer stole a look at Sarah but didn't correct the white lie. "You know she's missing, don't you?"

"I heard." Tara's face paled to an even lighter shade of white. "What do you want with me?"

"We think you might have information that could help us find Maggie. You may not think it's important or connected, but if you could just tell us what you know about Wayne Harrington's outside consultant. The one you wrote about in your note to Maggie—Dale Kitteridge—could be behind Maggie's disappearance."

"I've already said too much. If they find out I was the one who leaked the documents to Maggie, I might end up missing, too."

She swallowed and averted her eyes from theirs. "I think they already know. I've been getting calls in the middle of the night, but I can hear breathing before they hang up so I know someone's there. And a car that doesn't belong in the neighborhood keeps showing up. As soon as they see I've spotted them, they drive off."

The fear radiating from Tara was almost palpable.

Jennifer and Sarah exchanged glances, and Jennifer spoke first. "We know two policemen who could help protect you. We'd trust them with our lives," she added when Tara's expression told her she was about to object.

Tara's eyes leveled with Jennifer's for a long moment. "You'd do that? Ask them to help?"

"Of course."

"All right. You seem like someone I can trust and if you're really a friend of Maggie Larkin, I want to help. That's all I was trying to do when I got in touch with Maggie. It wasn't right what Wayne Harrington was doing, but nobody was doing anything about it."

"We've been able to piece together the bribes he paid for the zoning permits, and Harrington has a reputation for not being completely legit. What can you tell us about Dale Kitteridge?"

Tara took a deep breath and told them the rest of the story. "He came into the office a few times and met behind closed doors with the guys taking the bribes. A couple of the other staff whispered about him 'fixing problems for Harrington.' And one of them said he'd gotten in her face and hinted that he could make trouble for her if she didn't give him the paperwork he wanted."

She took a sip of the water before continuing. "I'd read Maggie's stories about how she'd uncovered corruption in other cases and thought she might be the only person who could expose this. I never thought it would end up hurting innocent people, especially Maggie." Tears were filling her eyes.

Jennifer reached across the table to place her hand on Tara's. "You were doing the right thing. That matters. No one blames you for Maggie's disappearance."

"We're not here to frighten you. We just want to find Maggie," Sarah added.

"There's one more thing that might help. Harrington and Kitteridge came in together one time. They didn't see me because I was scooched down behind a filing cabinet and when I heard them talking, I was too afraid to stand up."

"What did they say?" Jennifer asked when Tara hesitated.

"Harrington told Kitteridge to scout out a secure place near the lake for private meetings." She used air quotes to emphasize "secure place" and "private meetings."

"That's all I know."

CHAPTER 19

On the way back to Sarah's house, Jennifer called Dennis Smith and explained Tara's situation.

"I can't make any promises, but I'll see what I can do about having extra patrols go by her house."

"Thanks, Dennis. She's terrified and if they're onto her…"

"No need to explain. I'll get on it right now."

They returned to Sarah's office, much to Max's delight. Sarah pulled up business records and located Dale Kitteridge.

"He owns a heavy-equipment rental yard. There have been some complaints about safety issues, but they never got past the complaint stage. From the looks of them, he must have paid somebody off, because they should have ended up as citations. He's got a shell corporation set up. Let's see where that goes."

She switched to property records. "I may have found something." She turned to Jennifer who looked up from entertaining Max. "The corporation owns a cabin on Perry Lake. That might be where they took Maggie."

A chill ran down Jennifer's spine—part dread, part intuition. "Can you bring it up on a map?"

Sarah turned back to her keyboard and first typed the

address into a map query, then used the satellite imaging to display it on the screen. "I've got it."

Jennifer looked over Sarah's shoulder at the screen, a sense of excitement and apprehension blending together.

"I can't zoom in on it like with a street map but it looks pretty isolated. There's only a camp road leading up to it," Sarah explained.

Jennifer studied the image. "I'm not one hundred percent sure," Jennifer said slowly, her gaze fixed on the screen. "but I think that could be it. Something about it feels right. Or close."

CHAPTER 20

Unlike most nights when the atmosphere during the Club's dinner was upbeat, the air in the room was heavy. Even Reuben, sitting on one side of Eva's chair, and Ginger on the other, sensed the tension all around them. Jennifer and Sarah had just recounted their discovery of the real identity of Maggie's inside source and the location of Dale Kitteridge's cabin in the woods. Eva's face paled and Annalise was unusually quiet when they finished.

"Should we tell Phil and Dennis about this?" Eva asked. "They could send someone to rescue her."

"I think it's too soon, Eva," Sarah said, hating to knock down the hope she heard in Eva's voice. "We don't have anything concrete to link this to Kitteridge or Harrington."

"And I'm really not sure the satellite images matched what I saw in my vision. Going after them too soon could put Tara Greene in more danger, too," Jennifer said.

"She was terrified," Sarah noted.

"Dennis called me this afternoon to let me know he got permission for extra patrols to go by her house," Jennifer informed them.

Annalise had remained quiet during the exchange, nervously

rubbing her hand up her opposite arm. "I had a vision this morning," she blurted, and all eyes turned to her.

"I'm not sure if I was just channeling your vision about the cabin in the woods, Jen, but I agree that this looks very similar to what I saw," she said, placing her finger on the printout. "It was on the shoreline of a lake. I could see patches of ice through the snow at the edge of the water. Maggie was locked in a bedroom. She was huddled under a comforter and she was whispering 'Not here... not here...' She's strong, but she's really scared. I could feel it."

Eva sucked in her breath and Reuben jumped up onto her lap. Ginger's ears perked, and he sat upright, his eyes darting from Annalise to Eva. "What does that mean?" Her voice was soft and thready.

Annalise met her gaze. "I don't know, Eva. The connection wasn't strong enough. It could mean it's not the location we suspect or it could mean she's been moved." There was another possibility, but Annalise didn't want to go there.

"Where would they move her to?" Eva asked, panic rising.

"That's what we're going to find out, Eva," Sarah said and reached out to squeeze Eva's hand, hoping her physical touch would calm her. "Dale Kitteridge could have other properties and I'm going to track down all of them. Once I have that list, I'll turn it over to Phil and Dennis."

Reuben bumped his forehead against Eva's chin in a rare moment of sympathy and public display of affection. Ginger licked Eva's hand, adding his affection.

I could say you're just sucking up, Reuben said glancing down at the dog, *but Eva needs this, so I'm going to let it pass.*

If that's what you really think, I can't change that, but that's not what my intention is. Anyone can see she's upset. She's taken me in while Maggie's gone, and I'm grateful for that, Ginger replied.

Reuben looked into his eyes, judging Ginger's sincerity, gave a slight nod of his head, and curled himself in Eva's lap, purring as she stroked his fur. She stopped briefly to stroke Ginger's head and smiled. Reuben opened one eye to stare at the dog who recognized the challenge and lay back down on the floor snuggled against her feet.

Although she remained quiet, Eva was aware of their exchange and her shoulders relaxed. She hadn't been aware they'd risen nearly to her earlobes between the news about Maggie and ongoing stress of the feud between the animals. *Maybe this is the start of a truce between them,* she thought and hoped it wasn't wishful thinking.

"So where do we go from here?" Annalise asked.

"I'll keep digging into property records and look for any that are set up in a shell account's name. And I'll take another look at *all* of the files on the flash drive. I was going to do that this afternoon, but my day job demanded I do that first. Hashtag adulting." Sarah looked at Eva. "I really would have rather worked on this, but..."

"You don't have to apologize, Sarah. I completely understand. You're right to wait until we have more information to take this to Phil and Dennis. We don't want to waste their time going after false leads." Eva knew that was the right thing to do, but the fear she felt for Maggie warred inside her.

"I'll try to connect again with Maggie," Annalise offered. She hesitated, unsure about voicing her concern. "I'm worried we're running out of time." Her voice was quiet, and the words hung heavily in the air.

They were all painfully aware of the urgency.

"If there's anything I can do to help, let me know, Sarah," Jennifer offered.

"I don't know what I could do, but I'm willing to help," Eva added. "Anything at all. We need to get Maggie home."

There was nothing more to say or do for Maggie that night and the meeting shifted to their quilting projects.

Jennifer reached down to the bag on the floor beside her and pulled out a Friendship Star block. "I brought one of the blocks I made for Maggie's quilt. I wanted to do something a little differ-ent, so I've embroidered a paw print to add a dash of Ginger."

"Oh, Jen, that's wonderful! Maggie is going to love that special touch. What do you think, Ginger?" Eva asked.

Jennifer beamed at the praise and Ginger's ears perked up at the mention of his name. Jennifer held up the block for his inspection. "I had the idea it would symbolize him watching over her. I tried to find thread that matched the color of his fur." She reached into her bag again and pulled out a strand of embroidery thread, then held it against Ginger's fur. "That's a pretty good match, if I do say so myself."

Woof!

Eva smiled. "Ginger approves."

Of course he does, Reuben grumbled under his breath. He was still curled on Eva's lap and didn't even bother to lift his head to speak.

"Are you jealous, Reuben?"

This time he lifted his head to glare at Eva. *Of a dog? Some-times I think you don't know me at all.*

"Oh, I know you," Eva replied.

He narrowed his eyes at her and jumped down to remove himself from the room.

"Looks like you've insulted him," Sarah commented with a grin.

"For about the hundredth time just today. His skin is a bit thin."

I heard that.

Eva chuckled, but let him have the last word.

"Let's get the table cleared and move into the sewing room. Seeing Jennifer's block has me excited about getting more blocks done so we can finish Maggie's quilt."

No one needed to mention Annalise's warning. They all knew time was running out—and not just about finishing the quilt.

CHAPTER 21

"You've got to watch this. I haven't been able to stop laughing," Ashley said, her eyes still on the YouTube video on her laptop. Max looked up sleepily from his spot beside her and seeing Sarah, leaped from the couch to run to her. She knelt down to scratch under his chin with both hands as he closed his eyes and sighed blissfully from her affection.

"Maybe later. I have some work I want to do."

Sarah's serious tone caught Ashley's attention and her brows furrowed when she saw her expression. It wasn't like Sarah to be so serious after coming home from a Quilts Club get-together. "Rough meeting?"

"Yeah. Annalise thinks we're running out of time to find Maggie."

"Is it just a hunch or does she have something to base that on?"

"It's just a hunch, but with Annalise, I trust that it's real. I want to see if I can find any new leads from Maggie's flash drive."

"Can't it wait until morning? It's getting late."

"I don't think I could sleep even if I tried. You don't need to wait up for me."

"If there's one thing I know about you, Sarah, it's that once you get into 'dig mode,' there's no point trying to tear you away." Ashley's smile deflected any offense Sarah might have taken from the comment.

"You've got me there," Sarah said returning the smile. "I'm going to make some coffee and head up to my office. Just in case I'm too in the zone to hear you come upstairs, I'll say goodnight now."

"Goodnight to you, too. I'm probably wasting my breath, but don't stay up too late."

"No promises, but I'll do my best to get to bed before dawn breaks," Sarah replied.

Five minutes later she was ensconced in her office, a carafe of coffee nearby. Max had opted to remain with Ashley.

"All right, Maggie, let's see if you've got any other 'recipes' for me," she said, plugging the flash drive into a USB port. *Please be there*, she willed the drive to reveal a folder, a file—*anything*—that would give them some clue about where she might be held.

She spent the next half-hour scrolling through every file on the drive, but nothing jumped out. She started to see patterns in how Maggie organized her material, though. She sat back in her chair and played through the documents in her mind, searching for connections, but still nothing. And then smacked her forehead as she had an aha moment.

Maggie probably never looked into the cabin. She didn't have any reason to. She'd been digging into people and paper trails for the river-front *properties.* It embarrassed Sarah that it had taken so long to realize the obvious truth. "You're off your game, Pascal. It's time to move on."

She went back to the property records for the cabin. Between Jennifer and Annalise's visions and her gut, that was the most logical place to start. If that turned up nothing new, she'd move on to any other properties Kitteridge owned. It wasn't until she was reviewing the deed transfer that it occurred to her to search for the property listing by the realtor.

"Yes!" she exclaimed and pumped her fists in the air. The listing was still there along with photos and a property description.

She scanned through the details hoping for something meaningful that could lead them there. It was off-grid—powered by solar—so there wouldn't be any records about utilities. It was never intended to be a four-season camp and the wood stove appeared to be the only heat source.

Sarah then clicked on the photographs taken of the camp's interior and exterior. It was a typical seasonal cabin. She saw the solar panels on the roof and clicked through to the next photo, but felt a nudge to go back. *There's something mounted on that tree.*

She zoomed in and a tingle of excitement ran through her.

It's a web cam. There might be a way to access it.

It was a longshot, but she had confidence in her tech skills. If there was a way to hack in, she'd find it. She zoomed in closer. If she could identify the camera brand, she might be able to get in using the software. Even someone like Kitteridge might have been sloppy about changing the password.

The camera housing had a tiny QR code and a partial serial number printed beneath it. It was slightly pixelated, but she enhanced the section and the resolution cleared up enough that she was able to make it out. Her pulse quickened.

It was a TrailWatch SolarCam—a model she knew used device-based registration. If a camera wasn't claimed by an active account, the manufacturer's website allowed a new user to "reactivate" it through the device ID.

She opened a new tab, navigated to the spot to Add a new device and carefully typed in the serial number. She double-checked the number to make sure it was correct and held her breath as she clicked on the Submit button. A pop-up message immediately appeared on her screen:

This device has been inactive more than three years. Would you like to claim it?

She let out her breath in a whoosh.

"Yes. Yes, I would."

A new prompt appeared instantly: Your device is now activated.

Sarah's breath caught as she considered another problem—would it need a Wi-Fi connection? Given how seasonal and remote it was, the camp wasn't likely to have it. She searched: "Does a TrailWatch SolarCam need Wi-Fi?" The response was instantaneous:

TrailWatch SolarCams transmit motion clips through a low-powered cellular uplink, designed for remote camps without internet service.

With a little more digging she learned that it used a built-in LTE module to push motion clips to the cloud which made it perfect for off-grid cabins. Even those miles away from the nearest router. All it needed was a weak cell signal and enough solar charge to wake up when something moved.

It was too dark to see anything tonight and unlikely any human would be out to trigger the motion sensor. *Might as well get some sleep and wake up early to make sure it's working.*

She stretched her arms overhead, yawned, and shut down her computer. But the image of the cabin lingered in her mind long after she lay her head on her pillow.

CHAPTER 22

Ashley was dressed and ready to leave for work by the time Sarah came downstairs the next morning.

"Guess I overslept."

Ashley smiled. "A little. How late were you up?"

"It was about midnight, but it was worth it. As soon as I get caffeinated, I'm going back up to check that it works."

"What works?" Ashley asked, frowning.

"Oh, right," Sarah yawned. "There's a web cam at the cabin and I was able to reactivate it. I don't know if Kitteridge doesn't realize it's there or just doesn't bother with it. I'm hoping it's both."

"That's awesome! If it works, you'll be able to see who's there. Are you going to let the detectives know about it?"

"Not until I make sure it's operational and someone is at the cabin. I couldn't see anything last night—it was too dark. I need to get up to my office now. The second I see any sign of life—the *human* kind—I'm calling them."

"Good luck. I should be home in time for dinner. I started chicken soup in the crock-pot. See you later, Max. Be a good boy and don't let Sarah get into any trouble."

Woof!

"He's probably saying *Good luck with that.* He's not the boss of me. Isn't that right, Max? But you love me anyway." Sarah leaned down to kiss the top of Max's head. "And I love you right back."

Ashley simply rolled her eyes and left without another word.

Sarah filled a mug with coffee, turned to go to her office, then turned back again. "I might need this," she said, and took the half-full carafe with her. Max trotted behind her and plopped down on his bed that was perfectly located to catch the sunlight streaming through the window.

"Wish me luck!" Sarah booted up her computer and spoke a silent prayer beseeching the camera to work. She paused with her index finger poised above her mouse before finally clicking to wake up the web cam.

"Thank you," she whispered, and her shoulders relaxed when her monitor displayed a black-and-white image of a cabin in a clearing of woods. It was focused on the front door POV but extended out perhaps fifteen to twenty feet in front of the cabin. The snow was trampled by boot prints leading into the cabin, confirming someone had been there recently.

"We got it, Max!" she shouted loud enough to cause the dog to jump up from his bed and swivel his head side to side trying to find the reason for Sarah's outburst. "Sorry, boy. I got excited. You can lie back down."

Max gave her one last look before curling up on his bed.

Sarah debated calling the detectives. Yes, someone *had* been there, but it didn't mean they still were. "Why didn't you put the camera where you could see the whole cabin?" she muttered. "If I could see smoke coming out the chimney I'd know for sure someone was there."

Her stomach was in knots—she believed Annalise's prediction that finding Maggie soon was critical, but if she wasn't really there, she might be wasting time sending the police on a wild goose chase.

Sarah's eyes widened, and she sat at attention as the camera flickered but stayed on. Her eyes remained fixed on the screen as a doe appeared from the right side of the cabin. It sniffed at the snow in front of the door, but then continued its path into the woods on the other side.

"Well, at least I know it works." But disappointment tightened her chest just the same.

There was no sound, just video, and if she was distracted, she might miss something. She set up a push notification to alert her if the camera turned on again just in case.

An hour later she was deep into research for her day job when a notification popped up.

MOTION DETECTED — LIVE VIEW AVAILABLE

Her pulse spiked, and she crossed her fingers before clicking onto the camera app. It might just be the deer, but she couldn't risk not looking. The resolution of the camera wasn't great—the image was grainy, but it wasn't a deer.

Sarah froze as she saw a snowmobile slide into the frame and a man dressed in a puff jacket and a full helmet that obscured his features, got off and unlocked the door, then walked into the cabin. She continued staring at the screen, then shook herself and grabbed her phone.

"Phil, I think I've found Maggie," she said when he answered, barely able to contain her excitement.

"You saw her?"

"Well, no, but I've found the cabin where we think she's being held," she answered, her excitement deflating like a punctured balloon. This wasn't the triumphant *I found her moment* she'd imagined. Adding to her disappointment, her only response was dead air.

"Phil, you trust us, don't you? And you trust Jennifer and Annalise when they say they've had a vision?"

A weary sigh filtered through the connection. "Yeah, *we* do, but how am I supposed to explain this so they'll send officers out there?"

"You tell them you've had an anonymous tip... an informant

you've used before… I don't know… but I'm telling you, my gut says this is the right place. Please, Phil."

Sarah waited through another moment of silence and then heard another sigh. "All right, I'll see what I can do. Give me the coordinates."

After they'd disconnected, Sarah began a group text to let the ladies know about the cabin web cam but was interrupted by a ding alerting her she'd received a text message.

> Officers on the way. Should be there in twenty minutes.

Her first reaction was disbelief that he'd pulled it off and then a surge of relief. It would be over soon and Maggie would be back home. She deleted the text she'd been composing. *Wait until you have all the news and know that she's been rescued. You don't want to give them false hope.*

Sarah hated that voice of caution in her head, but knew it was the right thing to do.

The push notification for the camera pinged again, and she woke up her screen to watch.

The door opened and the man stepped out, his head was lowered so she couldn't see his face as he put the helmet on. He turned back to the door that was still ajar and instead of closing the door as she expected, he was holding onto the arm of someone else, leading them out of the cabin. The silhouette was female and her head was lowered, too. The man continued to hold on to her arm as though guiding her. His back was to the camera now, and he blocked Sarah's view of the woman.

She tried to zoom in, but the camera didn't budge. Then she remembered: it was a low-quality model—no sound, no ability to pan or zoom, just a single line of sight. She squinted at the screen and leaned in toward the monitor hoping to get a better view. Just as she did, the man turned to face forward and walked toward the snowmobile with his hand on the woman's arm, leading her.

"Oh, no!" Sarah cried out. The sight punched the air from her lungs. The woman was blindfolded, but Sarah knew it was Maggie. The man put a helmet on her and helped her onto the snowmobile, then sat in front of her to drive.

She dragged her gaze from the screen and frantically navigated to Phil's number.

"*Pick up. Pick up. Pick up,*" she implored as the phone rang once, twice, and then finally on the third ring, Phil answered.

"They're getting away! He's got a snowmobile with Maggie on the back." She sputtered in a panic, the words blending together as she rapidly spoke.

"What? Slow down, Sarah."

She took a deep breath and repeated her message, slowly this time.

"Do you know which way they're going?"

"No, the web cam only faces the cabin and they're going away from it. There's only one way in and out, though. It's a one-lane camp road from the looks of it on the satellite map."

Phil swore under his breath. "Okay, I'll let them know and get back to you."

A sick dread filled Sarah. Her brow furrowed as she shut her eyes and played the scene again in her mind, concentrating for any clues to identify the man or his snowmobile. It didn't help that the image was monochrome. The best she could do there would be that the man's jacket was dark and Maggie's was light.

Think, Sarah, she exhorted. She squeezed her eyes tighter, chasing details she knew weren't there. *Snowmobiles have stickers on both sides of the cowling. That's their license plate,* she remembered. As much as she tried, though, she couldn't see them. The snowmobile had been facing away from the camera when the man first arrived and they'd left in such a hurry, she'd been too shocked to pay closer attention.

The words "not here" popped into her head. It had been a warning. Annalise had been ahead of the events. She'd seen

Maggie in the cabin, but her foresight had been telling her she'd be gone.

"But she's still alive. They're just moving her," Sarah said aloud. She jumped when her phone buzzed in her hand. She saw Phil's name on the screen and answered with her heart in her throat.

"We were too late. They're gone."

The words cut like a knife. *I should have checked sooner. I should have dug into the cabin more. I might have noticed the camera in time.*

None of that mattered now. The only truth was: they were gone.

CHAPTER 23

"We should do this more often." Liam Campbell said. He and Annalise were at The Checkout Diner having a late breakfast. The Diner was warm and the smells familiar—bacon, onions, and toast blended with the aroma of coffee. Several tables were occupied by locals, mostly retirees at this time on a weekday and the clatter of silverware and quiet conversation provided a cozy backdrop.

"It is nice, isn't it?" Annalise and Liam had been dating for two months now and it was the first relationship since the death of her husband nearly thirty years ago that felt *right*.

Liam cocked his head to the left and squinted his eyes. "You seem a little distracted. You okay?"

"Sorry, I had a vision about Maggie Larkin a couple days ago and it's been nagging at me."

Glen Lake's chief gossip and server at the Diner, Betty Jones, appeared at their table, coffee carafe in hand and refilled their cups. "Have you heard any news about Maggie Larkin? Folks say she's missing, and it's got something to do with the Wayne Harrington trial."

Annalise recognized Betty's phishing attempt, but she was

telling the truth when she said, "Nothing new. She's still missing, and the police don't have any leads that I know of."

"Well, I hope she's all right. She comes in every now and again and is a real nice lady. If you hear anything, let me know."

"I will." Annalise smiled to be polite, but had no intention of adding to the rumor mill.

"Can I get you anything else?" she looked to Liam and then Annalise, but they both shook their heads. "Okey-Dokey. I'll be back with your checks, but you folks take your time. It's quiet today."

Liam watched the exchange and saw something in Annalise's expression that Betty missed. "Tell me about your vision," he spoke quietly once Betty was out of earshot.

Annalise's throat tightened, and she had to swallow to set the words free before she could recount the scene of Maggie huddled in the cabin. As soon as she mentioned Maggie's name, she felt a blast of cold air on her face and the room disappeared as though something was blocking her sight. She sat frozen, unable to move, staring straight ahead at Liam, her eyes empty.

Liam reached across the table to squeeze Annalise's hand. "Lise, are you okay?" He felt a rise of panic in his chest when she didn't respond at first. The thought, *She's either having a vision or a stroke,* flashed in his mind and he hoped it was the former.

Annalise shook her head to clear it and the room came back into focus. "Let's get out of here first. I don't want Betty overhearing."

Betty appeared at their table as though she'd been summoned and Liam reached out to take their check. Once they were settled into his car, Annalise continued.

"It's Maggie. I think she's blindfolded. I could feel wind on my face and I heard an engine start up—not a car, though. My head got heavy like there was something on it... it could be a helmet. It's just a guess, but I think she's on a snowmobile. That's the only thing that makes sense given where they're keeping her. She's scared, Liam."

Liam met her eyes and held out his hand and closed it around Annalise's.

"I'd heard her saying 'not here' in the last vision, but I didn't understand what it meant. It's clear now she was trying to tell me she's not at the cabin, but I think it just happened. When I saw her before she was still there. I should have seen what was coming."

"You weren't wrong. You know that sometimes what you see isn't literal, or the timing isn't the same as the present."

"I need to call Sarah. She was going to check on the cabin."

Sarah answered on the second ring and Annalise's stomach clenched when she heard the despair in her voice.

"They've moved her, Annalise."

Liam stole glances at her as he drove, his hands tightening involuntarily on the wheel, while Annalise sat stoically looking forward as Sarah brought her up-to-speed on her discoveries from the night before and that morning.

"Then it's true," Annalise said, barely above a whisper when Sarah finished. She cleared her throat and spoke again, her voice stronger. "I saw her this morning leaving the cabin. Everything you've told me confirms it. Where does this leave us?"

"I'm sorry, Annalise. We're back to square one. If we knew the real names of her abductors, I'd have a better place to start looking. All we have is the fake credentials they used when they took Maggie. I'm afraid they might not use another Kitteridge property if they think we're onto them."

"It's okay, Sarah. You did everything you could. It's not your fault we didn't find her in time."

"Logically I know that but I still feel guilty I didn't put it together sooner."

"Remember that saying, guilt is optional? Put it behind you and do your magic. I've got faith in you, Sarah. You've always come through on a case." *Hypocrite*, she thought. She was telling Sarah not to feel guilty while she was drowning in her own.

"Thanks, I needed to hear that. I should call Eva and Jennifer now to let them know what's happened. We'll talk later."

"That's something you need to tell yourself," Liam said when Annalise disconnected the call. "The one about guilt being optional."

"I know." Annalise's smile wasn't convincing Liam, but he let it slide.

They were both quiet, lost in their own thoughts. Annalise broke the silence a few minutes later. "I'm so glad we met. I'm feeling better and you're the reason why. In the past I would have still been beating myself up."

"I'm glad we met, too. So, you're okay now?"

"Yeah. I needed to process it, but I'm in a more optimistic place. My sixth sense is telling me not to give up. We're going to find Maggie."

Liam looked over and saw the conviction in Annalise's eyes. "I believe you."

CHAPTER 24

nnalise's pep talk had helped. Sarah was less shaky and ready now to call Eva and Jennifer with the news. She dialed Eva first.

"What's happened?"

"Hold on, Eva, I'm going to conference in Jennifer so I can tell you both at the same time," Sarah replied and switched to add a third person to the call. "Jen, I've got Eva on the line with us."

"What's going on?" Jennifer asked.

"Maggie's been moved." She caught Eva's sharp inhale of breath.

"Oh, no… Wait, start at the beginning and tell us everything," Jennifer said.

Sarah recited the events leading up to Maggie's departure from the cabin and her conversation with Annalise.

There was a moment of silence as Eva and Jennifer processed the information.

Sarah swallowed hard. "I'm sorry, Eva. I should have figured it out sooner."

"Nonsense. I'm not meaning to dismiss Jennifer and Annalise's visions, but you actually *found* Maggie. Now we know for sure that she's alive. So, you have nothing to be sorry about."

"I second that, Sarah. I saw her at a camp, but do you have any idea how many camps there are in Maine? We would have needed months… heck, maybe years… to figure it out and we don't have that much time."

"Thanks, guys. It's just that now we're back to square one."

"And we're still farther along than we would have been without your help. Now, let's put this setback behind us and move forward," Eva said, keeping her voice stronger than the worry squeezing her heart.

"We're going to find her. I believe that with all my heart," Jen added.

"It seems like Maggie would have had more notes about Kitteridge after Tara warned her about him," Eva reasoned. "There must be other names of the players helping Harrington."

"Maybe. I'll look through her notes again," Sarah agreed. Their reassurances had helped. She felt a flicker of the confidence she'd had before Maggie's removal from the cabin stir within her.

"That's my girl. Take Max for a walk. It will do you both good and when you come back, go through the drive again with fresh eyes," Eva suggested.

Sarah glanced out the window. It was cold outside, but typical for February. The sun was shining, though, and that always made the temperature seem warmer.

"That's a great idea, Eva. And thank you—thank you both— for talking me off the ledge. What do you think, Max? Should we go for a walk?"

As soon as she said the word "walk" he was up on all fours, tail wagging. *Woof!*

Sarah laughed. "He thinks it's a great idea, too. I'll get back to you when I find anything."

———

Eva had been right. The walk was just what she'd needed. Back in her office, she took a legal pad and began making notes. Sometimes the act of physically writing out the words instead of typing them helped her make other connections.

At the top of the page she wrote "Who are the players?" and wrote Wayne Harrington's and Dale Kitteridge's names. She'd been so focused on Kitteridge and his properties to find *where* Maggie was kept, she hadn't expanded the names to include his operatives and employees to narrow down the list of *who* might be likely suspects.

She opened the flash drive and went back to the "recipe" with Tara's note. There was a date written next to it that she'd disregarded before. If that was the first time Maggie had learned about Kitteridge being involved, any research into him would be dated after that. She began opening folders and scanned through the creation dates of the documents. She almost scrolled past it, but a sub-folder titled "Ginger's vet files" that was part of a folder titled K-Group was in the right date range. She hadn't opened it earlier because she assumed Maggie had misfiled it. The other documents in the folder had been copies of transactions between Wayne Harrington's corporation and Kitteridge's records as Harrington's general contractor.

Her fingers trembled as she double-clicked on the folder. Her heart sank when it revealed a list of documents, all labeled with Ginger's name on every file. Then instinct pushed her on. She looked at the dates—all of them were dated shortly after Tara's note. Her shoulders tensed as she clicked her mouse on the first document and then excitement flooded through her when she saw what was written.

At the top of the document was "K-Group Employees" and underneath was a list of names, sorted into subcategories: Independent contractors; Part-time labor; Seasonal workers. And then the one that made Sarah's heart race was the one labeled "Off-the-books consultants."

This could be it! Maggie's abductors could be one of the six names on the list.

CHAPTER 25

nderneath the list, Maggie had typed: "Full profiles in file named Ginger's vaccination records". Sarah opened the document and skimmed through Maggie's notes, taking in the clean formatting, the concise bullet points, and the occasional emphasis. She admired Maggie's organizational style—so similar to her own—and the breadcrumb trail Maggie had left. She began making her own notes on her legal pad.

Nolan Pike age 38

- Bouncer
- Lives in Bangor
- Arrested for assault - charges dropped when witness recanted

Troy Larrabee age 32

- Lives in Bar Harbor
- Finish carpenter who did "extra" jobs
- Had cash deposits matching suspected off the book jobs

Brenner Cobb age 45

- Lives in Old Town
- Runs small engine repair shop; fixes mostly snowmobiles, ATVs, generators
- Kitteridge used him for maintenance of his personal snowmobiles
- Often has financial troubles

Dean Ruhl age 41

- Lives in Brewer
- Consultant for several LLCs
- He's attached to Harrington's shady property purchases

Silas Dane age 39

- Lives in Brewer
- Former private security
- Has training in weapons and tactical removals
- Several payments received from Kitteridge related to Harrington's property purchases

Rowan Mayhew age 36

- No confirmed residence
- Possible fixer/"cleaner"
- No social media or public records
- Payments align with Harrington's shadiest deals
- MAGGIE HIGHLIGHTED HIS NAME

Sarah sat back and let her gaze travel down the list and crossed through Troy Larrabee and Dean Ruhl's names. They didn't fit as possible abductors.

She circled Brenner Cobb's name. He might not have been one of Maggie's abductors but the snowmobile connection alone put him high on any reasonable suspect list. She understood Maggie's logic for including him.

That left three.

She drew a question mark beside Nolan Pike's and Silas Dane's names and circled Rowan Mayhew's name several times. Since Maggie had highlighted his name, she must have believed he warranted special attention. Sarah agreed with her assessment.

"Okay. That's a good start. But *why* would they have moved Maggie? They didn't know anyone was looking."

She tapped the eraser end of the pencil against her lips, the soft, repetitive rhythm grounding her as Max flicked an ear in response. She considered and then wrote:

They somehow figured out we found the cabin.

She sucked in her breath. Had she tipped them off when she registered the trail web cam? For a moment fear surged—its unwelcome presence gripping her until she forced herself to slow down and think it through. *If they'd been using the camera, she wouldn't have been able to switch the registration to re-activate it.* That made sense. The system had let her in too easily for anyone to be monitoring it. The tension in her shoulders eased by a fraction.

The cabin was only meant to be temporary.

Maybe the abductors aren't on the same page. One of them is afraid? Consequences if they get caught?

•   •   •

She paused as an image she fought the urge to relive formed anyway—Maggie being hurried out of the cabin, blindfolded, and forced onto the back of the snowmobile. The panic that overwhelmed her when she saw them drive away. Sarah swallowed hard and refocused.

Who would have ordered the move? Abductors? Kitteridge? Harrington?

She's still alive because they need more information from her and don't want to risk her being rescued before they get it.

None of the possibilities were comforting, and they all pointed to the same conclusion: Someone who knew how to vanish when needed.

But which one?

Two of them stood out.

Brenner Cobb.

Rowan Mayhew.

A faint chill crawled up her spine as she circled the names. She needed someone who would have inside knowledge and instincts to verify her suspicions. It had to be the detectives.

"Did you find the guy on the snowmobile?" Phil asked after they'd exchanged hellos.

"No, but I found another one of Maggie's files with a list of names. I've narrowed down possibilities but I could really use your input. And maybe you could check them out more officially."

"I'm going to put you on speaker so Dennis can listen in." There was a brief pause. "Okay, we're ready."

"Do you want the whole list—there are six names—or just the ones I think are the most likely?"

"Give them all to us. We might have information you don't," Dennis said.

"I'll start with the names I tossed out." Sarah read the list for them. "And these are the ones I kept."

"I get why you picked Brenner Cobb. The snowmobile connection makes him a prime candidate. I might have kept Silas Dane on the list, but Rowan Mayhew is a stronger choice. I don't want to frighten you, but he's a really bad actor, Sarah," Phil cautioned.

"And he's slippery. We know he's guilty, but we've never been able to put together enough evidence to charge him with anything," Dennis added.

"Thanks, Sarah. We'll take it from here," Phil said.

They disconnected the call and Sarah sat motionless, staring at the names on her legal pad. The room was unnaturally still. The tick of the clock that most of the time barely registered in the background, now sounded like a metronome beating out its rhythm in the room. She replayed their conversation in her mind. She'd hoped sharing the information would ease some of the tension coiled inside her. Instead, the detectives' warnings about Rowan Mayhew had ratcheted up her fear higher—cold, and seeping into every fiber of her being.

Max sensed her mood and trotted over to her, placing his chin on her thigh.

It was enough to deflect her emotions and bring her into the present moment. She smiled at him and stroked his head. His soft fur comforted her.

"Thanks, Max. You always know just what I need."

CHAPTER 26

E va stared into the darkness of her kitchen window, her mind a million miles away. A thought had nagged at her all day—ever since Sarah's call to tell her about Maggie's list and her conversation with the detectives. Eva couldn't shake the sense that Sarah had held something back. And it worried her. *Did it mean Maggie was in more trouble than Sarah was letting on?*

She jumped at the sound of Jim's voice behind her. He'd seen the faraway look in her eyes.

"Is there something you'd like to talk about?"

"I'm fine," Eva protested.

Jim waited silently for her to continue—an interrogation trick from his days as a state police officer.

"You're doing that thing again," Eva said, scowling.

Jim chuckled. "Is it working?"

Eva huffed out a breath. "Yes. I know you won't let it go until I tell you."

"We'll both feel better once you do."

Eva sighed. "I know. It's Maggie—I'm feeling like I let her down. I'm the one she trusted to take care of Ginger if she had to go to a safe house."

"And that's what you're doing," Jim reminded her.

"But what if I had kept closer tabs on her? If I'd gone to visit her every day, maybe she wouldn't have been abducted because they'd know she was being watched."

"You must know you couldn't prevent that happening. Those guys were determined not to let her testify, and you couldn't be there 24/7."

"I know," Eva said, her voice resigned.

The tea kettle whistled, interrupting their conversation, and Eva poured the water into the teapot—the reason she'd come into the kitchen in the first place. Jim helped her with the mugs and pitcher of milk, and sat at the kitchen island while she made cinnamon toast. The aroma of bergamot and cinnamon was a homey, comforting presence. She placed the toast on the island and sat next to him.

"Think about all the people you've helped this past year. You —and the other club ladies. You're a team, so you don't have to take on all the responsibility. Maggie's going to come through this. The four of you won't let it play out any other way."

He gently set his hand on her shoulder. The warmth of his hand seeped into Eva, melting away the lump of icy fear and guilt that had settled into her.

"I hope you're right," she said with a half-smile.

Ahem.

Eva looked down at Reuben who was wearing the look that was half judgment, half demand for attention.

"I think he's trying to tell you that you've worried long enough," Jim said.

Reuben narrowed his eyes.

What I'm saying *is—where is* my *snack? The two of you sneaked off from the living room and here I find you, filling your faces.*

Ginger's toenails made a clicking sound on the tile floor as he walked into the kitchen.

And here comes the interloper.

Eva noticed Reuben's words didn't quite match his tone.

Something had shifted the past few days between them. Not that Reuben would admit, and Eva fully expected the snark to continue, but it didn't carry the bite it had when she'd first brought Ginger home from Maggie's.

"Actually, he's telling me he wants a snack and, in not so many words, that we are mistreating him." Eva raised both eyebrows at Jim and rolled her eyes to signal she wasn't buying it, but got up to get Reuben a snack, anyway.

"Here you go." She put a kitty snack in his bowl. "And for you, Ginger," she said taking down a bag from an upper cabinet, "one of your special treats."

Ginger immediately sat and waited for Eva to hold out her hand with the treat, then gently took it from her with his teeth. He devoured it in seconds. *Thanks*, he said, and looked at her with a hopeful expression in case it might win him another, but she'd already put the bag back.

A few minutes later Jim put the now-empty dishes in the dishwasher. "Ready for that movie now?"

"Born ready."

Jim smiled at the turnaround in her mood. The four of them trooped back into the living room. Reuben didn't waste any time inserting himself between them and raising a paw for his grooming regimen. Much to all their surprise, Ginger jumped up and plopped his head in Jim's lap. His back end partially covered Reuben. Jim and Eva both burst out laughing at Reuben's shocked expression—his tongue stuck halfway out of his mouth and his back leg was sticking up in the air.

Eva wiped tears from the corners of her eyes with the back of her hands.

"Oh, my goodness. Thank you, Ginger. I needed that."

Reuben retracted his tongue and put his leg back down on the couch. Much to Eva's surprise, he didn't jump off, though. He gave Ginger a haughty look and climbed onto Eva's lap, circled twice, then lay down and began to purr.

This time it was Eva's turn to look shocked. Jim reached out and gently pushed up her jaw to close her mouth.

"Looks like they've decided to be friends," he said, as he stroked Ginger's head.

Reuben opened one eye to glare at Jim, then closed it again.

"Or not," Jim said, chuckling at the cat's unspoken admonishment.

"No, I think you're right. Reuben just has to have the last word, and he's too stubborn to admit he might be warming up to Ginger."

This time, Reuben didn't object.

Jim turned on the TV and began streaming the movie. For the first time that day, Eva felt like she could breathe again. Tomorrow might bring another challenge. But tonight—in this moment—she could relax knowing she wasn't alone.

CHAPTER 27

I t had been another restless night for Sarah. She'd received a similar pep talk from Ashley that Jim had given Eva, but with less success at relieving her guilt. She'd rebuffed every reassuring phrase Ashley offered until realizing it was no use, Ashley had given up. Every time Sarah closed her eyes, she saw Maggie blindfolded, riding away on that snowmobile. That she'd seen Maggie being taken away with her own eyes hadn't helped.

She queued up an upbeat playlist and turned the volume up to drown out the ticking clock. It soon grated on her nerves, but she kept playing it because it was still better than the clock's noise. She needed the distraction. If by some miracle it improved her mood, that was a bonus. Her day job was first on the list of priorities for this morning, but the notifications for the trail cam were still on. The screen displayed the cabin, looking desolate and devoid of life. A thin layer of snow had piled up on the porch since yesterday, unblemished by footprints making the scene look even more abandoned. Forgotten.

She'd hoped whoever took Maggie might have brought her back later in the day after the officers cleared the scene. It had become a compulsion she couldn't resist yesterday, returning to the camera's display again and again—just in case. She had no idea how many times she'd refreshed the feed—maybe thirty? A hundred? Each time her only reward was her own growing dread for Maggie's safety. It was an exercise in futility, though, and today was likely to be a repeat. Each time she clicked, there'd been a moment of childish hope followed by the same letdown when nothing had changed.

Sarah took a sip of her coffee, grimacing when she realized it was already cold, flexed her fingers and got to work. The cursor blinked expectantly, as though mocking her inability to focus. She read the same paragraph at least three times, but none of it registered. *Get a grip, Sarah. You have to get this done today,* she reprimanded herself. Her reminder of the deadline forced her to concentrate. It was a complex project, and she'd become so involved, she almost missed the notification. Max's ears twitched first, but it was his soft whine—more insistent than the ping— that cut through her concentration. She followed his gaze to the separate monitor screen and the image of the cabin. Same old picture.

She was about to dismiss the interruption as Max chasing ghosts, but then sucked in her breath when a figure appeared at the bottom of the frame. Her eyes rounded and her hand froze on her mouse. She wasn't holding her breath, but it became shallow and shaky. It was a single man walking toward the camp. She guessed his height at possibly six feet, and appeared to have a beefy build, although the snowmobile suit he wore made it difficult to judge. He wore a black balaclava pulled on so that only his eyes were visible as he turned back toward the camp road, then turned and checked the perimeter of the camp.

Reassured he hadn't been followed, he walked toward the camp's door. Something about the deliberate way he scanned the tree line made her skin crawl. This wasn't a random curious visitor—his motions were purposeful. His every movement was confident, controlled, almost military in precision. There was no hesitation. No fear. He turned the knob and went inside as though he belonged there. He reappeared a moment later—fast, and from the looks of his eyes, despite the poor resolution of the camera, furious. Even from behind the ski mask, rage radiated from his posture—the stiff shoulders, the rigid jaw visible beneath the fabric. His fists were balled as he looked around as though searching for clues for how Maggie had escaped.

Sarah's stomach twisted. Whoever he was, he'd expected Maggie to be there.

She'd been transfixed by the scene and rubbed her face with the palms of her hands to clear the hold it had on her. When she looked at the screen again, the man tore off one glove and pulled out his phone, then began removing the balaclava. Her fingers hovered above the keyboard for half a second—long enough to curse herself before jolting into motion. She jabbed the screenshot keys—Shift, Command, 4—and dragged the cursor around the man's face. The image blinked onto her desktop. Not trusting her hand to stay steady, she took another—this time of his entire body. Then another. And another. She didn't want to miss even a fraction of the angles. This must be what private detectives felt like when they were staking out their targets.

Grabbing her phone, she called Phil.

"There's someone at the camp!" Her voice was an octave higher than usual and the words came out in an excited rush. Phil's muffled voice came through the line as he spoke to someone else, but she couldn't make out the words.

"I'm having Dennis alert the officers. How long has he been there?"

"He just came. He's talking on the phone to someone and he looks mad."

"You can see his face?" Phil asked.

"Yes. And I got screenshots." Sarah stared at the screen, barely blinking, willing the man to stay long enough for the officers to reach the camp. Her stomach lurched when he jammed the phone back into a pocket of his snowmobile suit. "Oh, no…"

"What's happening, Sarah?" Phil's voice was calm, but there was an edge to it.

Sarah exhaled softly. "I thought he was going to leave. He's off the phone now, but he's going back into the camp. I don't think he knew Maggie was gone, Phil."

"Can you send me those screenshots?"

"I'll email them. I took them on my desktop, so can't text. I have it, but it would save me time looking it up if you just tell me your email address."

She typed as he spelled it out. "It's on its way. I didn't have time to clean up the resolution, but I can do that later if you need. Your techs can probably do as good a job or better, though."

"Got i…"

"He's leaving!" Sarah interrupted. "He's wiping the door handle. That must be what he went back inside for. He was probably wiping off any prints."

The sight of him methodically rubbing the metal with his gloved hand tightened her chest. His movements were cold, calculated, and practiced. This was no spur-of-the-moment reaction. This was someone who understood what to do to cover their tracks. She felt goosebumps rise on her forearms.

He was already wearing his mask and walked briskly in the direction of the road into the camp.

Sarah muttered an expletive under her breath. "I wish this thing had sound. Are they anywhere close yet?" she asked Phil.

There was a pause as he asked Dennis to check. "Still at least ten minutes away. If he's on a snowmobile, I doubt they'll catch up with him. There's a trail only a couple hundred feet from the camp road. It won't take him more than a minute or two to get there."

Sarah began typing a search request into her browser. Her fingers trembled just enough that she mistyped twice. "I'm looking for it now." She scanned the results and found three possibilities. She narrowed them down to the most likely, but her heart sank when she zoomed out to take in more of the trail.

It wasn't just one trail. It was a network of interconnecting trails and worse—one led to a trail that had to cover at least a hundred miles to the north. Her hope collapsed like a punctured balloon.

She clicked the mouse, zooming out again and again, but there was no end to the lines marking trails and it began to resemble a nervous system radiating in all directions. A single snowmobile could disappear into that maze and be gone. Minutes or hours later they could be out of the county, out of the state, possibly even out of the country.

"It's not just one trail. He could be anywhere." Her voice reflected her disappointment.

"Don't give up yet. Because of you, now we have his picture."

Sarah knew his intention was to boost her morale but after they disconnected, she continued to stare at the screenshots. The man's eyes—cold, flat, determined—seemed to stare back at her from the monitor. It looked like a warning—*don't mess with me*. Fear pricked at the base of her skull. She should let the other ladies know what happened, but she didn't have it in her. Not now, anyway. She couldn't face giving them one more report that ended in disappointment.

Dragging her eyes from the photos, she returned to her day job project, but the words on her screen blurred together, forming nothing but meaningless shapes. Any hope of giving it her full attention was gone. She tried to force herself to type, but her mind kept drifting back to those eyes and the man's expression when he'd rushed out of the cabin. His rage.

Scenarios of his reactions played in Sarah's head. Maggie's disappearance hadn't just inconvenienced him—he'd looked furious. Sarah didn't know what he planned to do next, but her gut told her it wouldn't be good. Men like that didn't handle being crossed.

She would have to tell them soon and it was up to her to break the news. She didn't want them to hear it from Phil or Dennis. She was their friend, and they deserved better from her.

But for the moment—just this moment—she let the cursor blink on an untouched line of text while the screenshots mocked her as though saying *You lose again.*

And Maggie was running out of time.

CHAPTER 28

"Sewing machine—check. Casserole—check. Printout of the screenshots at the cabin—check. And purse—check. Okay, I think I've got everything." Sarah looked up from her inspection of the items she needed for the weekly Club meeting. "I feel like Scarecrow from The Wizard of Oz. The only other thing I need is courage."

Ashley shook her head and the corners of her mouth lifted. "You've got plenty of courage. It will be fine. They aren't going to be mad at you."

Max gently placed his paw on Sarah's thigh in solidarity as she slipped into her puff jacket and looked up at her with bright brown eyes. His gesture and Ashley's reassurance hit their mark and Sarah couldn't help but smile back at them.

"Thanks, guys. I needed that." She kissed Ashley's cheek, gave Max chin scratches, and gathered up her things. "I should be back at the usual time. The weather forecast isn't calling for any snow and the roads are clear so driving won't slow me down."

"Be careful anyway. There was some melting today. Watch out for black ice if they haven't sanded the roads."

"I will. See you later."

Her hand was on the doorknob, but her phone's ringtone from inside her purse stopped her.

"Could you hold this for me while I check this, please?" She handed the casserole dish to Ashley, then reached into her purse for the phone, still ringing. "It's Phil."

Her stomach clenched. "Hi, Phil. I hope you have good news."

"I guess that depends. Probably more like good news, bad news. Which do you want first?"

"I could use some good news," Sarah replied.

"Okay. We don't have an address, but the good news is that our techs cleaned up your screenshot and we've identified him as definitely being Rowan Mayhew. That could be in the bad news column, too, considering his reputation. But at least now we have a suspect to go after."

Sarah hesitated. "Okay. If you don't have an address, how do you plan to find him?"

"There's an APB out for him as a person of interest in Maggie's abduction. And we've got the Warden Service involved. They're going to patrol the snowmobile trails and check on any camps Mayhew or his accomplice could be using to hide Maggie."

That planted the seed of an idea in Sarah's mind for research she could do after tonight's meeting. It would give her something productive to cling to that she was making a difference.

"Maine doesn't have a lot of traffic cameras, but we're using all we can to spot him and track his movements for the past week," Phil continued. "We might get lucky with private security cameras, too. That's all I've got for now, but I wanted to keep you updated."

"Thanks, Phil. And to Dennis, too. I know this isn't your case, so we really appreciate the help."

"You're welcome. Malone and Fitzpatrick appreciate it, too.

We told them we had a confidential informant who would only work with us, so they aren't pushing to have us reveal your identity. That keeps us on the case."

Ashley looked on as Sarah's expression brightened, making her own mood brighten as well.

"What about the other guy—Brenner Cobb? The one who we assume took Maggie?"

"Nothing on him either. We don't have anything we can bring him in for, but we're watching him. If he's got Maggie stashed somewhere, he's either working with someone else or left her alone. He's been working his usual hours at his shop today."

Sarah's brow furrowed. What if they were focusing on the wrong person?

Phil sensed her concern. "Dennis and I agree with your assessment, Sarah. We're focusing on him as her abductor, but we haven't ruled out other possibilities."

Satisfied with his reply, Sarah thanked him and ended the call.

"This time I mean it," she said, taking the casserole back from Ashley. "At least now I can tell the ladies what the police are doing to find Mayhew and Maggie."

As she drove to Eva's house, Sarah thought more about the camps the Warden Service would be checking on. She could make her own list of possibilities that might help Annalise tap into. She wasn't sure if that's how it worked, but she would ask.

Annalise and Jennifer had already arrived and were in the dining room. Their mood was light, as was Eva's, but it felt *off*. Sarah sensed their undercurrent of worry. Their posture was slightly rigid and there was an air of tension in the room. *I hope my news doesn't make that worse*, she thought as she joined them.

It only took a few minutes of chit-chat before Eva broached the subject of the most recent visitor to the cabin. That solved Sarah's dilemma of how and when to bring it up. She placed the printout of Rowan Mayhew on the table for them to observe and told them about Phil's call.

"Lise, if I gave you a list of possible locations where they might be holding Maggie, do you think you would be able to use your psychic skills? To figure out if they're a match, I mean?"

Annalise didn't hesitate. "It's worked before. I can't make any promises," she said looking directly at Eva. She hated the thought of giving her false hope. "but sure, I can give it a try. Send me as much information as you can about each location."

"I'll do that first thing tomorrow."

She's still alive. Reuben was sitting on the floor beside Eva's chair.

"How do you know that?" Eva asked, startled both by his presence and his announcement.

Isn't it obvious? If she was a ghost, she'd have appeared to Sarah.

Eva's jaw dropped. "Reuben just told me Maggie's alive. He thinks if anything happened to her, her ghost would have shown up to Sarah."

Sarah shook her head in amazement. "Why hadn't I thought of that? Reuben, you're a genius."

It's not like that's news to me, he said, giving Sarah one of his slow blink looks.

She's alive? Ginger appeared at Eva's elbow, almost stepping on Reuben who glared up at him.

Watch where you're going! Reuben growled, moving over to avoid being trampled.

Sorry, buddy. I got excited. Ginger leaned down and to his horror and humiliation, licked Reuben's face.

That's it! I'm out of here. Reuben trotted out of the room and up the stairs to his new hiding spot.

Eva watched the scene with amusement and once Reuben was gone, turned her attention to Ginger. "That's what we believe, Ginger. We haven't given up hope and Reuben made a good point. Sarah hasn't had any visits from Maggie. That's a very good sign."

Jennifer had been quiet during all of this, but broke her silence. "Why would this guy Mayhew have shown up at the cabin if he already knew she'd been moved?"

"We don't think he did. I saw the way he moved before he went into the cabin and his expression when he came out. He was extremely angry and immediately got on his phone. I'm almost certain he expected her to be there," Sarah replied.

Annalise drew the printout closer and studied the man's face. The room went out of focus and she caught a faint whisper *Where are you taking me?* She caught the scent of pine and the sensation of cold air on her face. Then the sound of footsteps crunching in snow. *Somewhere safe. Mayhew doesn't know about this place.* Annalise blinked twice as the vision ended.

"It was Maggie's voice at first. She was moved to keep her safe."

"From Mayhew?" Jennifer asked.

"I think so. There was another voice—a man's—telling her Mayhew wouldn't know where to find them."

"Given his reputation, that fits. Could be the other guy—and my bet's still on Brenner Cobb—didn't want to be involved if Mayhew thought the cops were getting closer. Mayhew doesn't seem like the type to leave any witnesses." The words were out before Sarah realized how they would sound and instantly regretted it. "I'm sorry, Eva," she said seeing the look on Eva's face. "I shouldn't have said that."

Eva shook her head and patted Sarah's hand. "I know you didn't mean any harm, dear. We were probably all thinking it. It just was a shock to hear the words out loud."

"If you need any help with the property search, Sarah, let me know," Jennifer offered. "We insure a lot of the camps on the lake, so we might have details about them or even photos if we were asked to do inspections."

"That's a great idea, Jen. I hadn't thought of that angle," Sarah said. "I'll send both of you the list of possible candidates tomorrow."

The evening passed with the mood being genuinely more upbeat. Reuben's revelation about Maggie being alive was just what they'd needed. Unlike earlier, Sarah's drive home was full of optimism and she couldn't wait to dig into the maps and property records tomorrow. But tonight, all she wanted to do was go to bed and get a good night's sleep.

CHAPTER 29

S arah woke refreshed and eager to get to her office. After a hasty breakfast and visit with Ashley before she left for work, Sarah ran up the stairs with Max right on her heels.

She found her legal pad buried under a pile of paperwork on her worktable and began jotting down notes for the research. The act of methodically listing them by hand, and organizing them into concrete steps, eased some of the residue of tension that hung on even after the restful sleep. Every so often she would pause to consider what needed to be added to her list, and once she was satisfied she had enough to begin, she sprang into action.

The first step would be examining the snowmobile trails map. She'd bookmarked the site the day before and opened her browser. The screen lit up as the map appeared and the tension she'd thought was gone tightened like a vise in her neck. The sheer size of the area it covered was incredible. She'd also found a travel-guide type article about Maine's snowmobile trails. She'd only bookmarked it then, but opened a new browser tab to read it. If the information in the article was accurate, just the groomed trails covered over 4,000 miles of interconnected pathways.

"You've got to be kidding me!" she exclaimed loudly enough to make Max jump up from his bed and trot to her side to make sure she was okay.

"It's okay, buddy. You can go back to sleep," she told him and gave him a chin scratch as extra reassurance. He licked her hand and walked back to his bed, circled it once and plopped down.

Sarah groaned when she read there were an additional ten thousand miles of secondary trails. "It's okay, Max," she said quickly when his head popped up to deflect another trip to her side.

"There's no way I can check all of these. I'm going to have to narrow it down."

She set the filter on the map to view the trails within a twenty-five-mile radius of Bangor and Glen Lake. It didn't make sense to her they would have gone beyond that but, if necessary, she could always expand the search later.

Next, she filtered them by camp roads connected to a main road with a snowmobile trail within a half mile based on Phil's account of Mayhew's getaway. Both Jennifer and Annalise had seen water nearby. It hadn't been visible with the trail cam but snow would have disguised its presence.

Max looked up sleepily from his bed at the sound of Sarah tapping the eraser of the pencil on her note pad as she formulated details for another criteria. Not all camps would be vacated in the winter. Some were even used that time of year for recreational activities such as snowmobiling, cross-country skiing, snowshoeing, and ice fishing. Whoever took Maggie would want privacy. She wrote *find camps that are hidden from direct sight by neighboring camps* on her list.

"No. No. No. Not. Now!" she said, her voice raising with each word.

That earned another visit by Max, but this time Sarah only distractedly stroked his head without taking her eyes from her screen. She repositioned the mouse and tried to refresh the now frozen window. "Of course, it has to freeze when I don't have time to waste. Just close it out and start over," she muttered to herself when her attempts were unsuccessful.

"Yes! That's more like it." Her shoulders relaxed when the page loaded and functioned correctly.

It took more time than she'd estimated, but after two hours, she had a list of ten possibilities. There was one more that might be promising but although there were coniferous trees on either side of the camp road blocking it from sight, it had a neighboring camp on the adjoining lot. It might not be secluded enough, but her gut was telling her it should be added to the list, anyway.

"Trust your intuition. You know it's served you well and you don't want to be sorry later if this turns out to be important."

She included as much detail as possible including property owners, their locations, and pertinent URLs in case either Jennifer or Annalise wanted to see them for themselves. She read through the list one more time and satisfied there was nothing more to add, she emailed the information to Jennifer and Annalise, then followed up with a text telling them to check their email.

It was out of her hands for now and she still had day job duties on the back burner. She opened up the files needed to work on the project, but couldn't fully concentrate on the data. A part of her brain was on alert, waiting for the ping notifying her of a response from one or both of the ladies.

Max appeared at her side with his favorite tug toy in his mouth and placed it on her thigh. This time Sarah did glance over and laughed out loud when his eyes shifted from her to his toy and then back at her again. His way of saying, "play with me."

"Okay, you win! Maybe a little break will be just what I need." She took the toy in her hand and held it out for Max but pulled it back just before he could snatch it. Max pranced in front of her, bending down with his hind quarters raised, and then jumping back up again to bite at the toy. This time she let him grab it and the game was on.

Meanwhile, in Glen Lake, Annalise and Jennifer were reading through their email from Sarah, each ready to do their best to connect the dots from Sarah's list to the most likely candidate.

CHAPTER 30

Annalise printed a separate page for each of the properties on Sarah's list and took them with her to her bedroom sitting room. Tension fluttered in her stomach, worrying her that she might not be successful. She turned off the lights, lit a candle and incense, and—old school—put on a CD of spa-type music to calm herself and set the mood.

For a few minutes she sat still, taking deep breaths in and out, until she felt as though she was in a warm cocoon, separated from the "real" world, and knew she was ready. She took the first printout off the stack and held her palm over it, moving it slowly across the page, tuning in her senses for any change—scents, tingling in her body, temperature, or images appearing. Nothing.

She worked her way through the stack, becoming more and more discouraged as each page had the same results. Anxiety gripped her chest whenever the thought *Maggie is counting on me* slipped through her cocoon. Each time she would acknowledge the thought and then release it and focus again on being in a state of relaxation.

Doubts became louder, though, and she wondered *Am I*

blocking this? Is something else blocking it? Is this just not a good day to receive messages?

Annalise took several more steadying breaths, then picked up the last page and felt a flutter of excitement, immediately followed by the thought it had been too easy.

Am I really sensing more warmth there or is it just wishful thinking?

She concentrated on the sensation, checking for her own emotional bias, and concluded, *Yes, it's weak, but it's definitely emanating warmth.*

With her eyes closed to eliminate any outside distractions, she slowly moved her hand to different places, and each time was rewarded in just one spot. She opened her eyes and removed her hand. No matter how many times she moved her hand to other spots, it always became warmer directly over the image of a camp located at the far end of Pushaw Lake. *So close!*

This time when she closed her eyes and put her hand slightly above the page, she held an image of Maggie in her head. Nothing changed for several minutes and then images rippled like water after a stone has been tossed into it. They were joined with sounds—muffled and distorted. Annalise focused on them, willing them to materialize into something she could grasp onto.

A sensation of fear gripped her stomach.

It's Maggie.

Her brow furrowed in concentration as she sought to strengthen the connection and then felt a jolt.

Annalise was suddenly inside the main room of a camp and she knew she was looking at it from Maggie's point of view. She was sitting on a couch, reading a book that she'd found in a bookcase. A fire was visible in the Vermont Castings wood stove. To her right, an eat-in kitchen occupied the space in the camp's open concept design.

A man was sitting at the table with his back to Maggie. He was hunched over the table, talking on his cell phone. Annalise strained to make them out, but the words were garbled. Maggie sneaked furtive glances at the man.

She's afraid, but not of him, Annalise realized.

The man's hair was dark brown with a small bald patch at the crown. It was difficult to judge his height from his seated position, but Annalise noted his stocky build. He wore a red flannel shirt with a gray quilted vest over it.

He placed the phone on the table and sat staring out the kitchen window ahead of him as though contemplating the conversation just ended.

Annalise held her breath as he turned toward her/Maggie. His silhouette revealed bushy eyebrows, a large hook nose, and thick lips.

Just a little more... Just a little more and I'll be able to see all of your face...

With a sensation of being yanked backwards, Annalise was fully in her sitting room again—her connection broken. She shook off the momentary confusion she felt and realized the ringing of her cell phone was the source of the interruption.

Arrgh, she growled, angry with herself. She couldn't believe she'd forgotten to turn off the phone. Even worse, the number was likely a spam call. She tossed it back down on the side table in disgust. The connection with Maggie was broken.

More time had passed than she thought. The candle had burned down so that the wax was pooling around the wick and about to snuff it out. She blew it out, pulling back her head to avoid the swirl of smoke curling up into the air.

She picked up the printout—still in her lap—and realized all was not lost. This was the place where Maggie was being held. There was no doubt in her mind.

Annalise picked up her phone.

"Hi, Annalise," Sarah's voice sounded in her ear.

Annalise's voice was clear and strong as she replied, "I found her."

CHAPTER 31

"What's on your agenda today?" David asked Jennifer as the two of them were finishing breakfast. Matthew and Nicole had left for school just minutes before.

"I'm going to the Town Office this morning. Sarah found some properties where Maggie might be held and three of them are on Pushaw Lake."

"If you already know where they are, what are you hoping to find out there?"

"If anyone knows the backstory of what's not on the public record, it will be Carline Mosely."

David chuckled. "You've got that right. Betty Jones may be the Diner's town historian, but Carline is the town office's. Well, I'm off. Have a good day and good luck! I'll see you tonight and you can tell me all about it."

"Thanks, babe. See you later."

Jennifer cleaned the kitchen and gathered up the printouts before leaning down to say goodbye to Boscoe who was taking his after-breakfast nap. He looked up sleepily when she patted his head, then closed his eyes and went back to sleep, relieved when he realized his assistance wasn't required. He'd already planned several hours of quality nap time in his agenda.

The Town Office was empty of visitors when Jennifer arrived. She glanced at the notice bulletin board in the entryway out of habit. The Congregational Church was hosting a baked bean supper fundraiser on Saturday. *That could be fun. I'll have to remember to ask Dave if he'd like to go,* Jennifer thought, making a mental note to follow up.

Carline Mosely had been employed as a town clerk for the last thirty years. Her personality was perpetually upbeat, and she kept her ear to the ground for any morsels of gossip to store in her mental information bank. She was short, plump, and had a riot of curly brown hair that always looked as though it was on the brink of breaking free of Carline's attempts to constrain it.

"Good morning, Jennifer. What brings you in today?" she asked, her voice cheery from the other side of the peninsula that separated the common area from the office.

"I have three camps I'm trying to find more about. I was hoping you could help me," Jennifer replied.

Carline's eyes lit up with more enthusiasm than the task warranted, but Jennifer presumed the prospect of digging into private properties tapped into Carline's need to be the voice of authority.

"Do you have the parcel numbers?" Carline asked.

"Right here." Jennifer handed her the printouts which Carline shuffled through before bringing back the plot maps in the bound journal stored in a bookcase.

"Looks like they're all at the far end of the lake. Not as much development up there yet," she commented before looking up at Jennifer. "You looking to buy? Might be a good time to get in before prices go up."

"Just exploring possibilities for now," Jennifer said, saying a silent thank you. Carline had given her the perfect excuse to justify her research.

Carline opened to the page for the first listing and slid the journal over to Jennifer. The neighbors on either side appeared too close to fit the criteria, but she kept examining it to avoid questions about why she'd dismissed it so soon. "How about the next one?" she asked when she thought it was safe to move on.

Carline flipped pages until she found the right one and they repeated the process.

"Should I call you Goldilocks?" Carline teased when Jennifer asked her to look up the third property.

Jennifer looked at her, confusion clear on her face. Her brain had already raced ahead, and she failed to connect the dots to Carline's reference due to her distraction.

"Like the three bears. Those two didn't fit but maybe this third one will," Carline explained.

"Oh, yeah. Now I get it," Jennifer said, but her expression hadn't been as convincing as Carline expected.

"Must lose something in translation," she replied drily as she pushed the journal toward Jennifer.

Oops, Jennifer thought. *I'll need to do better with this one.*

But as she examined the layout of the lot and the abutting ones, a tingle of excitement ran up her spine. The lot was bigger than its neighbors, giving it more opportunity for seclusion. And it checked all the boxes for the other parameters Sarah had listed.

"What can you tell me about this one?" she asked.

"Oh, that's the Cooper place. They've owned the property since the forties. It's owned by the grandson now. Nice guy, but he doesn't use it much these days. He's in a retirement home," Carline added.

Jennifer's excitement ramped up, but she kept her demeanor impartial.

"Does he let anyone else use it?"

"Yes," Carline said, warming to the subject. "His grandson comes out now and again, mostly in the summer and when we have our Fourth of July BBQ. We have a camp on this lot." She pointed to one two lots away.

"Do either of these have camps on them?" Jennifer asked pointing to the ones on either side of the Cooper property.

"Not yet. They might be good ones to follow up with. Do you want the owners' information?"

Jennifer nodded before Carline could ask anything more that Jennifer wasn't prepared to answer. "Sure, but first, what can you tell me about the grandson who uses the Cooper camp? It's important to have good neighbors," Jennifer said, smiling and giving Carline a conspiratorial wink.

"Don't you know it! You don't have anything to worry about with Brenner, though. He's a good guy. We take our snowmobiles out to him for maintenance. He has a shop in Old Town."

Jennifer's pulse quickened. "Brenner?" she asked, hoping she didn't sound too curious.

"Brenner Cobb. He's a good worker, but doesn't always use good judgement. Some people think he might be mixed up with that Dale Kitteridge, but he's never been anything but nice to us. You don't have to worry about him as a neighbor."

The mention of the Kitteridge connection wasn't a pairing she wanted to hear, but it was one more clue that tied them together. One that would help when they turned over their discovery to Phil and Dennis.

"Well, thanks, Carline. This has been very helpful." Jennifer gave her a parting smile and turned to leave.

"Wait! Don't you want the names of those other owners?" Carline called after her.

Better say yes if you don't want her getting suspicious.

"Oh, right. Good thing you're on top of things. And could I get a photocopy of this page so I can show Dave the actual plot plans?"

"We'll have to charge you a dollar," Carline cautioned.

"No problem. I'm happy to pay for it."

She waited impatiently as Carline made the photocopy and then wrote the owners' names on a slip of paper. She needed to get to her car so she could call Sarah but made herself remain calm.

At last, she was in her car nearly bursting with excitement. Just as she was about to call Sarah, her phone rang. Jennifer couldn't help but smile when she saw who it was.

"Hold on just a sec. I'm going to patch in Annalise. I have her holding on the other line," Sarah said.

Jennifer waited and exhaled in relief when Sarah came back on the line.

"We've got some exciting news to share," Sarah said as soon as she returned.

"So do I! You go first."

"Annalise figured out where Maggie is being held," Sarah announced.

"Is it the Cooper property?" Jennifer asked.

There was a moment of stunned silence before Annalise asked, "How did you know?"

"It's the same one I found. Carline Mosely told me that it's owned by his grandfather which is why the property ownership is in the name of Cooper. But get this, Brenner Cobb is the one who actually uses it!"

CHAPTER 32

There was a pause after the women had shared the details of their psychic and physical searches, as if each was waiting for the other to volunteer to call the detectives. At last, Sarah made the decision.

"I think you should be the one to call Phil and Dennis, Jen. You have the conversation with the town clerk to back up why we think that property is where Maggie is."

"You're right, that does make sense. I'm still in the parking lot of the Town Office, but I'll head home now and call them as soon as I get there."

"Keep us posted."

"I will," Jennifer replied, and backed the car out of the parking space. She needed to get her notes organized first, but as she drove, she rehearsed her conversation with the detectives.

By the time she returned home, Jennifer had the gist of what she wanted to say thought out. She sat at the kitchen table, jotted her talking points on the back of Carline's note, and placed it beside the plot plan and tax record printouts. She uncapped the yellow highlighter she'd taken from the junk drawer and ran it along the lines marking the Cooper camp.

The house was still quiet, other than Boscoe who was softly

snoring in the corner of the kitchen. She looked it over one last time before picking up the phone with her finger poised above Phil's name in her Favorites list.

What if I'm wrong? What if it isn't Brenner Cobb and I'm sending the police after an innocent man?

Her hesitation only lasted seconds as logic reminded her it was the best lead they had so far, and the stakes were higher for Maggie. She'd never forgive herself if she chickened out and they didn't find her in time because of it. And, she reminded herself, it's the same property Annalise identified as where Maggie was being held.

That was all she needed to remove any doubts. Jennifer tapped the Call button and took a deep breath to settle her nerves as she mentally repeated the mantra *This is the right thing to do* over and over until Phil picked up.

"Ryder residence—or should I be saying Quilt Club Hotline?"

At first Jennifer was lost for words at Phil's greeting, but quickly recovered.

"This time it's the Quilt Club Hotline and I have a hot tip that could wrap up this case."

Phil's tone was serious this time as he asked, "What have you got for us?"

Jennifer gave him her report, paraphrasing her notes to avoid sounding as rehearsed as she felt using her office "professional" voice rather than their usual exchanges.

"Can you email me the paperwork you have?" Phil asked when she'd finished.

"Sorry. I should have done that before I called so you'd have it." Jennifer used her phone to snap photos of the documents. She cursed herself as the first one turned out blurry. She hadn't realized how much her hands were shaking. This time she made a point to hold her hands steady and satisfied with the results, emailed them.

"No worries. Dennis is just walking back into the office. Why don't you do that while I bring him up-to-speed?"

"Already done. You should have them in your inbox." Jennifer straightened the papers in front of her, needing something to do with her hands.

There was a pause and then Phil came back on the line.

"I've got them. Dennis is here now, too. I have you on speaker."

Jennifer listened as Phil gave Dennis the information, interrupting once to expand on what Phil said. Dennis asked more questions about the road access and whether officers would have any difficulties driving to it.

"You won't need snowmobiles to access the camp. There's a snowmobile trail that connects to the road but there are some year-round residences beyond the Cooper camp, so the town keeps the road plowed," Jennifer explained. "This isn't something you'll be able to pass along, but Annalise tapped into this property before she had the information I got from the Town Office."

"We'll keep that to ourselves," Dennis said, "but if the two of you have landed on the same camp, that's all we need to make the calls to get this going."

"Is it going to be enough to send officers there?" Jennifer asked.

"It's an abduction so we should have enough using exigent circumstances to check it out," Phil said. "We can't sit on it. If we're wrong, we apologize. If we're right, we save a life."

Jennifer's eyebrows raised as she listened. *Exigent circumstances — that's something I never thought I'd hear outside of watching a TV show.*

"And one more thing we have to thank you for. Once we had Mayhew's name, we were able to get the DNA testing bumped up on that cigarette wrapper you found. They ran it through CODIS, and it's a match. Then they matched a partial fingerprint to one they found inside Maggie's house. It gave us enough to push through an arrest warrant for him," Phil told her.

A thrill of excitement bubbled up and Jennifer was all at once light-headed with relief. "That's fantastic! Have they found him yet?"

The bubble popped when Dennis replied, "Not yet, but we're running down some leads."

"We need to get this to the team. We've only got a few hours of daylight left."

Jennifer realized Phil was addressing Dennis, but her stomach fluttered as anticipation mingled with fear. *This could either be Maggie's rescue or…* She stopped herself. She wasn't going to allow negative thoughts and doubts to enter.

She was brought back to the moment when she heard Phil telling her, "We'll let you know when we've got news we can share."

After they'd disconnected, Jennifer couldn't take her eyes off the plot plan, as though willing her to be there so she could be rescued. And sent prayers for her safety. It was Boscoe's nose nudging her arm that brought her back to the room.

She smiled down at the dog. "Any suggestions for what we do while we wait?"

Woof! Woof!

She couldn't translate his barks into English the way Eva could, but they were what she needed to move her to action. The first thing she had to do was let the rest of the Club know what was happening, beginning with Sarah and Annalise.

She placed the three-way call and gave them the recap, including the news about the DNA match to Mayhew.

"I'd forgotten about that," Sarah said. "That was a great find, Jen. It's just the piece we needed to link him beyond a doubt to Maggie's abduction."

"I agree. So glad you followed your instincts and didn't just ignore it as trash," Annalise added.

"Thanks! Hold on, I've got a text coming in from Phil." She

scrolled to her text messages and read the message aloud so Sarah and Annalise could hear.

> Units en route to Cooper camp now. I'll update ASAP.

Annalise's sigh of relief was audible to the others and mirrored their own reactions to the news.

"I need to call Eva. She doesn't know any of this yet," Jennifer said and they said their goodbyes.

Please let Maggie be there. And please don't let it be too late, she beseeched, and then tapped Eva's name.

"Hello?"

"Eva, it's Jen. I've got news about Maggie."

CHAPTER 33

*Y*ou can't give up hope, Maggie told herself. Weak winter morning light filtered through the curtains covering the one window in the bedroom where she lay staring up at the ceiling. She hadn't slept well between the constant state of fear she'd been in since her abduction and the lumpy mattress on the bed.

Her attention was drawn to someone stirring beyond the closed door. Pots rattling, the aroma of coffee, and bacon frying meant Brenner was making breakfast. She'd managed to form a "relationship" with him. Watching all those TV shows with negotiators using first names to make hostages seem real to their abductors had come in handy. They'd left her suitcase at the other camp when they'd switched locations, so he'd even brought toiletries and some changes of clothing for her. They weren't high quality, but they were new.

Maggie had lost count of how many days had passed since she'd been taken from her home. Worry crept in as she thought of Ginger. *He's okay. He'll be with Eva and she'll be taking good care of him.* That felt true and although it wasn't completely gone, her anxiety lessened and her breathing relaxed.

There was a knock on the door, but Brenner left it unopened.

His voice—flat and terse from the other side announced, "Breakfast is ready."

Maggie debated ignoring him, but her stomach grumbled in protest and she swallowed to soothe her dry throat. She tossed aside the bed covers and swung her legs out from under them and sat upright. She stayed there a moment, her head down, trying to draw strength to face yet another day of captivity. *At least you're still alive.* It wasn't the most comforting thought, but for the moment, it was enough. She stood and walked resignedly into the main living space.

Brenner was sitting at one end of the table and opposite him, he'd set a place for her. The plate was already filled with bacon, two fried eggs, and a slice of toast. Steam rose from the mug of coffee beside it. Maggie's stomach grumbled again as the scents set off her hunger alarms.

Brenner glanced up as she approached and offered a weak smile. Maggie noticed the bags under his eyes and worry lines crisscrossing his forehead. *I'm not the only one who isn't sleeping well,* she thought.

After trying to engage him in conversation and only receiving monosyllabic responses, Maggie gave up and ate her meal in silence. She stole glances at him, noting how distracted he was, as though he was working out a solution in his mind. *He's spiraling,* she realized.

Once she'd finished breakfast, she washed her dishes and placed them in the drainer on the counter. Brenner was still picking at his meal.

"I'm going to go back to the bedroom and read for a while."

"Yeah, whatever," he replied, not even glancing in her direction.

Maggie's chest tightened as her sense of unease grew. *Something's happening or is about to happen.* She felt it in her bones.

Brenner remained sitting at the table after Maggie left. He stared out the window, his hands clasped tightly around his mug. The coffee had turned cold, but he didn't notice. His right knee bounced under the table as he considered his options.

Taking Maggie away without telling Rowan had been a mistake. It had been an impulse. He knew what Rowan had planned for her and he didn't want any part of it.

"This is bad. This is so bad," he muttered. "I never wanted this. It wasn't supposed to turn out like this. If he finds us..." He didn't want to finish the sentence aloud. He knew what would happen the moment Rowan had ordered him to "clean things up," but saying it out loud made it more real. "That's not what I agreed to," he said, muttering again.

The edge in Brenner's voice alerted Maggie that something was off and she crept to the door, pressing her ear against it. She could hear his voice, but he was speaking too quietly to understand the words. She turned to walk back to the bed, then froze as his voice became louder.

"Rowan, it's Brenner. We need to talk. Things changed. Call me."

Maggie sucked in her breath. *This could mean either that Brenner wanted to convince Rowan they needed her still alive, or...* She swallowed hard and a chill ran down her spine. *Or, he realized Rowan had been right about making sure she didn't talk—to anyone, not just in court.*

She crept back to the bed and tucked her knees up to her chest, wrapping her arms around them in a protective posture. Brenner's phone rang, but this time when he spoke, she could make out his words. She held her breath and focused her hearing to catch them.

"We're at my grandfather's camp."

Silence.

"Yeah, she's here. She's fine."

Silence.

Maggie's entire body tensed knowing Brenner must be talking to Rowan.

"I thought I heard somebody sneaking around the other place. I was afraid we'd get caught if we stayed there."

Silence.

"Yeah, we'll be here. But Rowan, we need to talk. I didn't sign up to hurt anybody."

Silence.

"Rowan? *Rowan?*"

Maggie jumped at the clattering of something being dropped hard, as though it had been slammed down.

Footsteps approached the door and her heartbeat raced. Brenner knocked once, then opened the door without waiting for her reply, but remained standing in the threshold.

"We're going to have company."

"What's going to happen?" Maggie asked, leveling her eyes on his.

His eyes flickered briefly. "I don't know. I'm trying to figure it out," he answered honestly.

"You don't seem like you want to hurt me. But what about Rowan?"

"I don't. That's not what I was told would happen." He paused, and she saw the uncertainty in his eyes. "I can't make any promises, but I'm going to do whatever I can to make sure Rowan doesn't hurt you either." He gave her one last look, then closed the door behind him and she caught what sounded like the turn of a lock. She tiptoed to the door and slowly turned the handle. It wouldn't budge. He'd never locked her in before.

Maggie had already tried the window shortly after they'd arrived. It was nailed shut. The only other escape was through the living room and the one door to the outside. There was no way out without being seen. She suddenly felt chilled to the bone, and tiptoed back to the bed where she crawled under the covers, tucking the comforter under her chin. *Think, Maggie, think! There's got to be a way out of this.* But she came up empty-handed as the minutes ticked away as both she and Brenner waited for Rowan to arrive.

In the living room, Brenner rehearsed the rationale he planned to use to sway Rowan from hurting Maggie. A half hour later, a car pulled into the driveway and he braced himself.

At the same time, the sound of tires crunching on snow snapped Maggie to attention. A car door slammed shut and rapid footsteps followed. The front door opened, and the bed shook slightly from the force of the door slamming closed.

Meanwhile, Brenner set his shoulders when the door yanked open and Rowan—his face contorted with rage—strode into the room.

"You had ONE job!" Rowan's roar took up all the empty spaces in the camp. His anger was palpable to Maggie even through the closed door of the bedroom. Maggie cringed and pulled the comforter even tighter as she listened to their conversation, any thoughts of escape or rescue dwindling rapidly.

"It wasn't to kill anyone," Brenner said, his voice stronger than he felt.

Rowan advanced on him, grabbing the front of his shirt and placed his nose nearly touching his own.

"Where is she?" Rowan hissed.

Brenner's resolve wavered seeing the killing rage in Rowan's eyes.

"I told you she's here." He nodded his head toward the bedroom. "She's not going anywhere. She's locked in."

"I'm getting her out of here. I can't trust you to take care of this," Rowan growled.

———

Maggie tensed, expecting Rowan to storm in. Her heart thudded in her chest as the seconds ticked off, but no one appeared. Thoughts of home, of Ginger, flashed through her mind and the idea that she might never see either again, made her stomach clench.

The silence was suddenly broken by a voice outside.

"STATE   POLICE!   STEP   OUTSIDE   WITH   YOUR HANDS UP!"

Maggie's breath caught in her throat as she sat bolt upright and tears welled in her eyes. *This was it. She was being rescued.*

Her elation was quickly quenched when she heard the door being unlocked and it swung open. Rowan marched to the bed and yanked at her, but her feet tangled in the covers. He gripped her wrist tighter and pulled again before she had time to recover. This time, she was drawn out of the bed, her knees buckling as she almost fell to the floor.

"Get up!" he yelled at her.

Maggie got her balance and Rowan pulled her behind him into the living room where Brenner was cowering in the kitchen.

"Pull those curtains shut," Rowan demanded, pointing at the windows in the kitchen, as he gripped Maggie's upper arm to hold her close.

Brenner hurried over and pulled at the curtains, but they didn't slide easily, and he had to repeat the motion to move them along.

He turned back to face them once he was done and Maggie locked her eyes on his, beseeching him silently. Then mouthed, "Don't let him hurt me."

Turning to Rowan, she said, "You don't want to do this. There's still a way out."

"Not for me," he snarled, tightening his grip on Maggie's arm, making her wince.

"Stop it! You're hurting her," Brenner shouted. "She's right. We can fix this."

Rowan looked at him incredulously. "Are you serious… or just stupid? You really think they're going to let us just walk if we hand her over?" He barked an ugly laugh.

Brenner knew in that moment, it wasn't just Maggie whose life was in danger. Rowan meant to eliminate them both.

All eyes turned toward the sound of the voice outside repeating, "WE KNOW YOU'RE IN THERE. JUST COME OUT WITH YOUR HANDS UP AND NO ONE WILL GET HURT!"

"Come on, Rowan. Jail time for kidnapping is still better than murder. We were just doing what Kitteridge and Harrington ordered."

"SHUT UP!" Rowan screamed at him. "I told you there's no way out of this. We won't be safe even in jail." His nostrils flared and his eyes bored into Brenner's as he spoke.

Rowan shoved Maggie onto the couch and pulled a gun out of the holster strapped to his chest beneath his jacket.

"You, over there with her," he said to Brenner, gesturing with his gun hand toward the couch.

Maggie tracked his movements, barely daring to breathe, as he paced back and forth, raking his free hand through his hair.

"Rowan. Cobb. You are surrounded. Send Ms. Larkin out. We can end this all safely today."

This was a different voice—a negotiator's voice, Maggie thought.

Rowan stopped pacing and stood with his back to them, staring at the front door with his gun cradled in both hands, as though he expected the officers to break through.

"Don't move," Brenner whispered in Maggie's ear.

She turned to him, her eyes round, as she comprehended what he intended to do.

Brenner cautiously raised himself off the couch and crept toward Rowan. A floorboard creaked just as he got within a foot of Rowan. He whirled around, his eyes wild, and pointed the gun at Brenner, but before he could fire Brenner tackled him. They both fell backward, and the gun discharged a bullet into the ceiling.

Maggie watched in horror as the scene played out. The blast of the gun echoed inside her skull, freezing her in place.

The door splintered open with the force of the battering ram hurled against it and officers swarmed in. Brenner and Rowan were still struggling on the floor, Brenner's hands gripped around Rowan's wrist to keep him from using the gun. The officers pulled Brenner off and secured the weapon as they forcibly restrained Rowan. Another cuffed Brenner who allowed the restraints to be placed on his wrists without resisting. His shoulders sagged—defeated.

An EMT rushed to Maggie, who was shivering uncontrollably from the cold air rushing into the camp through the doorway and the release of adrenalin from finally being rescued.

"Bring in a blanket," he told his partner. "You're all right, ma'am. We've got you."

Her ears were ringing, and she was unable to speak at first. The shock of the last few minutes was all too much for her to handle. The EMT kept his voice calm as he spoke, forcing her to focus on him and away from Rowan and Brenner being escorted out of the camp.

Phil and Dennis walked in once the scene was secure. Phil knelt down at Maggie's eye level.

"We know some people who are going to be very happy to hear you're okay." He took his cell phone from his pocket and tapped the number in his contacts. "I have someone I think you're going to want to talk to," he said, when a voice answered and he handed the phone to Maggie. "It's Eva," he explained.

"Eva?" Maggie asked, her voice tentative.

"Maggie?" Eva replied, not quite believing her ears.

Tears rolled down Maggie's cheeks as from the other side of the call, Eva was doing the same.

CHAPTER 34

The detectives and EMT gave Maggie a few moments alone while she spoke with Eva. When the call ended, she frowned at the phone in her hand. "Whose phone is this?" she murmured, more to herself than anyone in the room.

"It's mine, ma'am," Phil said gently as he took it from her. "My name is Detective Robertson, and this is my partner, Dennis Smith. We're friends of Eva Perkins and her other quilt club friends. They helped us find you."

"How's she doing?" Dennis asked the EMT, who had draped a blanket around Maggie's shoulders and was finishing his exam.

"All things considered, she's doing very well. She doesn't need to go to the hospital."

Another man stepped forward.

"I'm Agent Fitzpatrick," he said and held out his ID. The name sent a jolt through Maggie; she searched the detectives' faces for assurance.

Phil understood immediately and nodded once. "He's who he says he is," he spoke quietly. "He's here to take you to the real safe house. Dennis and I will follow behind to make sure you get there safely."

"I can't go home?" Maggie asked, her shoulders drooping.

"Sorry, ma'am," Agent Fitzpatrick said with quiet sympathy. "Until you've given your testimony, we'll need to keep your location secure."

Maggie nodded, resigned. She pushed up from the couch. Her knees wobbled. *Stand straight. You're going to walk out of here on your own two feet.* The pep talk steadied her. She waited a moment, anchoring herself.

"Thank you," she said turning to address each of the men in the room. Her eyes shimmered, but no tears escaped.

A female officer appeared at her side with Maggie's jacket, which the officer had found in the bedroom. "I'm Officer Davidson. You're going to want this instead of that blanket." She held out the coat for Maggie while she slipped her arms in.

"Thanks," Maggie said gratefully.

She followed Officer Davidson and Agent Fitzpatrick outside to the waiting car. Before getting in, she turned and exhaled deeply as she took one long last look at the camp.

During the drive, Maggie was hyper-aware of the landscape they passed by. She tracked landmarks along the way—*just in case*. Every so often, she turned to look out the rear window to make sure the detectives were still there. Twenty-minutes later, they turned into one of the newer subdivisions in Bangor and pulled into the driveway of a two-story Colonial. Agent Fitzpatrick used the remote to open the garage door and guided it in, lowering the door behind them before turning off the ignition.

Phil and Dennis cruised past the driveway and circled the neighborhood to check for any suspicious cars parked nearby before leaving, satisfied she was secure in the house.

"I'll show you to your room, Ms. Larkin," Officer Davidson said, leading the way to an upstairs bedroom. "We recovered your suitcase from the first camp where you were held and brought it here earlier so you'll have your own clothes to wear."

Relief flickered through Maggie at the sight of the familiar bag. "Thank you so much. I think I'd like to lie down for a bit, Officer Davidson—if that's okay."

"Of course. And you can call me Sandy," she said warmly.

Maggie smiled. "In that case, please call me Maggie."

Once alone, Maggie surveyed the room, relieved to find an en suite bathroom. She placed her suitcase on the bed, chose a clean outfit from the freshly laundered contents, and walked to the bathroom. She turned the faucet on full and stepped in, steam rising around her.

Thank you, she whispered as the water poured over her and washed away the remnants of fear still clinging to her.

Later, Maggie was jolted awake by a knock on her door. She sat up disoriented. She didn't know how long she'd slept, but the room was now only dimly lit.

"Maggie?" She relaxed when she recognized Officer Davidson's—Sandy—voice gently calling from the other side of the door.

It all rushed back to her—the rescue, the drive to the safe house, and then relief—*it's okay, I'm safe now.*

"I'll be right out," Maggie replied.

"We have dinner ready if you're hungry."

Her stomach let out an embarrassingly loud rumble, making Maggie smile. "I'm on my way down."

There was an extra person at the dining room table—someone she recognized—Sylvia Collins, the prosecutor for the Wayne Harrington trial. During their previous meetings, Sylvia had always been reserved and professional. To Maggie's great surprise, Sylvia rose and wrapped her arms around Maggie. "I'm so glad you're safe. And not just because of the trial," Sylvia said before releasing her.

"Thank you," Maggie said, touched. "It's all a little surreal, but I'm glad it will be over soon. When will I have to testify?"

"We've arranged to have you present your testimony tomorrow," Sylvia told her. "But you won't have to be in court. We convinced the judge that it would be much better to do this with a Zoom meeting. Given what you've been through, there was no argument."

"Really?" Maggie could hardly believe her ears. "You can do that?"

"You're scheduled for nine o'clock."

"And then it will be over? I can go home?"

Sylvia hesitated, and Maggie knew the answer even before she spoke.

"We think it best to wait for the jury's decision, but we're hoping that won't take long. The evidence you uncovered is strong."

Maggie deflated a little, but understood the delay. At least by tomorrow her part would be over.

"I thought you might like a home-cooked meal," Sandy spoke up, shifting the attention away from the trial. "Judging from all the fast-food wrappers we found at the cabin, you've probably had your fill of that."

Maggie groaned. "I don't think I'll be able to eat pizza for at least a month. This looks amazing."

And it was. After being prepped by Sylvia for her zoom testimony, Maggie returned to her room. Despite the nap she'd taken that afternoon, she was asleep almost the instant her head touched the pillow.

CHAPTER 35

E va stood, frozen in place, her phone still clutched in her hand.

It's finally over—Maggie's alive. She's safe.

She had to repeat the words several times until they became real.

Ginger nudged her knee, bringing Eva back to the room. She gripped the island to steady herself and sank onto the barstool. Waves of emotion crashed over her—relief, then tears, followed by shaky laughter.

Ginger cocked his head when she looked down at him. Reuben sat a few feet away, a bewildered look on his face as though he thought she'd gone mad. That only made her laugh more.

"They found her! Maggie's safe," she explained.

Ginger's tail wagged furiously, putting his entire back end in motion, and he barked joyously as he pranced at Eva's feet.

When can I see her?

Before Eva could reply, her phone rang again. It was Phil, calling from his car as they followed behind Maggie. She listened as he filled in new details about Maggie being taken to a safe house and answered Eva's questions about Maggie's condition.

"What about Mayhew and Cobb?"

"They're on their way to the county jail. They're going to be segregated from each other. Dennis had a chance to interrogate Cobb."

Dennis took over the conversation.

"Cobb was in way over his head. He had no idea it would go so far as to harm Maggie. I won't be surprised if the DA's office offers him a deal once he gives his statement."

"You mean he'll go free?" Eva asked, her voice raising in indignation.

"No, no. He won't walk away from this. It's not up to me, but my guess is he'll get a reduced sentence. Mayhew won't be as lucky."

"Good! After what he tried to do to Maggie, he doesn't deserve to see the light of day."

She thought she heard a low chuckle from Phil in the background, but let it pass.

"She must still be scared to death. Are you sure she's okay?" Eva asked.

Phil gently reassured her of Maggie's condition. "She'll have two officers with her and extra patrols."

"Okay," Eva said, nodding her head, satisfied with Phil's response.

"We'll keep you updated when we hear anything," Dennis told her before disconnecting the call.

Eva pressed the phone to her chest and Ginger rested his chin on her lap. Reuben turned on his heel, bored now that the excitement was over.

"She's safe, Ginger, but she can't come home yet."

He whined softly and gave her sad puppy-dog eyes.

"It shouldn't be long, boy," she said, stroking his head.

This time instead of a call, she sent a group text.

> Maggie's been rescued. She's okay. Will tell you all about it at tonight's meeting.

Responses came immediately from the others.

SARAH

THAT'S AWESOME!

ANNALISE

That's such a relief! Can't wait to hear the deets. ☺

JENNIFER

What wonderful news! I'm even more excited to see you all tonight. ♥

Everyone was in a celebratory mood when they gathered at Eva's dining room table for the meeting.

"I've been on tenterhooks all day long about tonight!" Annalise exclaimed.

"What the heck are tenterhooks?" Sarah asked.

"Tenterhooks. You know—on the edge of my seat. Nervous anticipation," Annalise replied, smiling. "Guess I'm dating myself with that one."

"It's okay, Sarah. I wasn't sure what that meant either," Jennifer confessed.

"I'm glad to know it wasn't just me. Moving on. Tell us what happened and don't leave anything out," Sarah addressed Eva.

Eva relayed the information Phil and Dennis had given her, stopping to answer their questions, and the news that Maggie would be testifying via Zoom the next day. "And then she can come home," she wrapped up.

It seemed as though the room itself let out a collective breath of relief along with the ladies.

Ginger's ears perked up, and he trotted over to lick Eva's hand. "Soon, buddy. Very soon you'll be back with her."

Woof!

"I swear he's smiling," Jennifer said, as Ginger curled up on his bed in the corner of the room.

"Can you blame him?" Sarah asked, smiling too.

Jennifer shook her head slowly. "Not at all."

"So tonight, we need to put the quilt sandwich together so I can do the quilting and bind it. I was thinking we should have a party with all of us and our partners and Maggie and Ginger, too, to celebrate her homecoming."

"Are you sure you'll have time to get it done?" Annalise asked, skeptically.

"If I have a week, that should be plenty of time. But I'll make sure it's done even if that means putting aside everything else."

"I can make the binding for you tonight. That will save you a little bit of work and time," Jennifer offered.

"Thank you, Jen. Actually, that would be a big help. I won't get too fancy with the quilting—just an overall edge-to-edge pattern would still be very pretty."

"Maybe Quilting Essentials would have time free to rent their quilting machine," Sarah suggested.

"That's a great idea! I'll give Evelyn a call tomorrow," Eva replied. "Does next Friday evening work for all of you to have the party?"

"Works for me," Annalise said. "I'll need to check with Liam, but if he can't come then, I'll come by myself. I don't want to hold up the celebration."

Jennifer and Sarah checked their calendars.

"Should work for us," Jennifer said. "With all of our commitments to keep track of, we have a family calendar and for once, there's nothing scheduled for a Friday night."

"I'll double-check with Ashley, but put us down as a yes," Sarah told them.

"Excellent! Now, let's get this quilt sandwich put together."

Did someone say sandwich? Reuben asked as he strolled into the room.

"Unless you like eating quilt batting, it's not the kind of sandwich you think it was," Eva replied.

Reuben glared at Eva and twitched his tail, then trotted back to his cushion.

By the end of the evening, the quilt was pinned together and ready for the decorative quilting and Jennifer had cut and sewn together the binding. It was coiled up next to her sewing machine, ready for Eva to attach.

"There's one last step before you go—the label." Eva presented a quilt label and gave each woman a fabric marker to sign their names. "Now you can go," she said when they'd finished.

Eva waved goodbye as they each backed their cars out of her driveway and then closed the door, resting her back against it for a moment as she felt a sense of peace.

Tonight I can breathe again. Maggie's safe.

CHAPTER 36

The next morning Maggie awoke early, the room illuminated by shafts of sunlight. She couldn't say how long she'd slept, only that the exhaustion had run deep. Today would be a challenge, but in a different way—she was safe, and she faced it knowing it would soon be over.

She dressed and went downstairs to review her notes one more time. The aroma of coffee and baked goods greeted her as she descended the stairway. She closed her eyes briefly, inhaling not just the scent, but the sense of comfort and safety it carried with it. Sandy, Agent Fitzpatrick—Allen—and Sylvia were gathered at the dining room table and looked up when she entered the room.

"Good morning. Are you ready for today?" Sylvia asked.

"I think so, but I wanted to go over my notes again."

"You're going to be fine. This isn't the first time you've been a witness at a trial," Sylvia reassured her.

"Never one quite like this, though. Am I going to have to see Harrington's face?"

"No. The camera will be positioned so you're facing us, not him. I'll make sure of that," Sylvia told her.

"Good," Maggie spoke barely above a whisper. She felt her shoulders ease.

They passed the next hour prepping and Maggie's nerves settled. She was ready. She'd do her part and hope it was enough to convince the jury, but that was out of her control.

"I have to leave now. I'll be in court, but right here with you in spirit," Sylvia told her, giving her a brief hug before leaving.

Agent Fitzpatrick had set up the equipment in the home office area and Maggie took her seat behind the desk, taking several deep breaths. Fitzpatrick opened the email from Sylvia Collins and clicked on the link for the Zoom meeting.

"You're on," he told her when the connection was made and the image of the courtroom appeared on the screen. She was sworn in and the trial began.

She was shaky at first but her confidence rose as Sylvia's eyes met hers and she nodded imperceptibly each time Maggie responded to a question, letting her know she was doing fine. Maggie's face set with determination. *This is your chance. Tell the truth. Take him down.* She kept her answers short and to the point and her voice became stronger with each response. Despite Harrington's lawyer's attempts to trip her up, Maggie answered his questions with factual statements defending her claims of Harrington's guilt regarding the bribery and corruption charges.

It lasted over ninety minutes. Once the call ended, Maggie slumped in her seat, wrung out with emotion.

"You did great," Allen told her as he broke down the equipment.

"I agree." Sandy had been watching off to the side out of camera shot, and brought Maggie a glass of water once she knew it was clear.

Maggie gulped down half of the glass, her hand trembling slightly. "Thanks. Now what?"

"We wait," Allen replied.

The waiting didn't take long. To all their surprise, Sylvia called less than two hours later.

"It's over," she said, her voice uncharacteristically giddy. "The jury found him guilty!"

A flood of relief flowed over Maggie. "Does this mean I can go home now?"

"Yes," Sylvia said, a smile in her voice. "You can go home."

CHAPTER 37

I t was the next day before Maggie could go home. Bureaucratic paperwork had held things up. It was only one more day, but the waiting felt even longer than her time in captivity. Determined that it would be her last day at the safe house—even if it meant calling a taxi—Maggie packed her few belongings in her suitcase. It gave her a sense of regaining control. As an independent, self-sufficient woman, that aspect of her captivity had been almost as difficult to bear as fearing for her personal safety.

Soft steps ascended the stairway and Sandy came to her doorway. "Allen and I need to go over a few things and there's one more document…"

"I thought we were done with the paperwork," Maggie interrupted, her tone coming out more tersely than she intended. *Don't take it out on her; it's not her fault.* "I'm sorry. That was uncalled for."

"It's okay. I can only imagine how hard it must be for you when all you want is to get back into your own house and to be with your dog again."

Maggie gave a wry smile. "If I know Eva, she's been spoiling him rotten. He may not even want to come home."

"I don't think you have anything to worry about. It's more likely he won't let you out of his sight for at least a few days. Not until he's sure you're not going anywhere without him."

"That's a problem I won't mind having," Maggie said, zipping up her suitcase.

"Can I take that down for you?" Sandy asked.

"I've got it." Maggie set the bag on the floor and extended the handle, ready to follow Sandy downstairs. *There it was again—not wanting to give up control.*

Allen was sitting at the dining room table. In front of him was a thin stack of papers stapled in the left top corner and a pen.

At least it's not as thick as the paperwork I had to fill out yesterday, Maggie reasoned. *I might just get out of here by noon,* she thought, and took the seat opposite him.

"Sylvia just called and gave us the thumbs up to take you home. She'd forgotten to have you sign the final release form earlier," Allen said sliding it over to Maggie.

Maggie read through the document and signed it.

"We'll be having unmarked cars as well as patrol cars checking on you. I know this may seem like an imposition, but if you could text either me or Sandy if you have plans for guests or you need to leave your house, that helps us avoid assuming something's wrong when it isn't."

When he read Maggie's expression, he rushed on, "It's only until we're sure Harrington isn't going to try anything."

Maggie raised her eyebrows, questioning Allen's logic. "He's not that stupid. He knows he'd be the first person you'd look at."

"You're probably right, but we don't want to take any chances."

Maggie sighed. "All right. I get it. But I need to get back to having some normalcy in my life and that doesn't include feeling like I'm a teenager again who has to let her parents know where she is every minute of the day. How long will I have to keep doing this?"

Allen and Sandy exchanged glances as they silently debated their answer.

"A week?" Allen said, but it came out as a question for Sandy to confirm. She nodded. "A week," Allen said, decisively that time.

"I'm not crazy about it, but okay," Maggie said. "Can we go now?"

"Absolutely," Allen replied.

Maggie watched the familiar scenery pass by. Its normalcy felt out of place somehow. She realized she wasn't returning the same person as the one who'd been abducted from her home. She became aware of an undercurrent of anxiety worming itself into her gut that grew more insistent the closer they got to her house. The memory of her abduction hovered in the back of her mind.

When they pulled into her driveway, Maggie remained seated in the passenger seat, taking slow breaths to calm her nerves. *Is this what PTSD feels like?* she wondered. It wouldn't be surprising. She'd been through a traumatic experience and being here where it started, triggered the response. *Is this how it will be every time?* It scared her to think so.

Allen had already stepped out of the car but Sandy was still in the back seat. Allen leaned back in to speak to Maggie. Her face was composed, but pale. "Sandy's going to wait here with you while I go inside to check things out."

Maggie's shoulders relaxed. *It would be okay. No boogeymen would be hiding in the closets when she went inside.* She nodded. "Thanks," she said, gratefully and handed him her key.

It wasn't long before Allen came back to the car and Maggie rolled down her window.

"It's all clear," he told them and walked to the trunk to get her suitcase.

Maggie and Sandy followed him into the house. He set the suitcase down beside the stairway.

That's the same spot where I'd put it, Maggie thought, but didn't dwell on it. Instead, she walked slowly through the downstairs rooms as a need to check them herself compelled her, while the officers waited patiently in the foyer.

"We can wait a little longer if that would make you more comfortable," he offered. "Sometimes people are still shaken up even after everything is over."

"No, thanks. I'll be fine."

Allen noticed the color had returned to her cheeks. It was a good sign.

"In that case, we'll be on our way." He held out his hand, and she took it, her hand firm in his.

Instead of a handshake, Sandy wrapped Maggie in a warm embrace. "You have our cards. If you need anything—anything at all—just call."

"Thanks. I will," Maggie replied, and meant it.

Maggie still felt a sense of unease once they'd left but recognized it for what it was. She needed Ginger back with her. She had a moment of panic when she couldn't find her phone but found it at the bottom of her purse, not in its usual spot in the inside pocket. She tapped Eva's number, and a smile stretched from ear to ear at the sound of Eva's voice.

"I'm home, Eva."

"Oh, that's wonderful, Maggie. I'll get his things together and bring Ginger home. He can't wait to see you."

Maggie swallowed the lump in her throat. "I can't wait to see him, too."

————

Eva gathered Ginger's food and toys in a shopping bag and carried them, along with his dog bed, and placed them in the trunk of her car. Ginger followed her every move and sensed that something was happening.

Am I going home? Eva noticed the cautiousness in his voice.

She ruffled his fur on either side of his face with both hands and smiled. "Yes, Ginger. You're going home. Maggie's waiting for us."

Ginger broke free and ran to the garage door and back again when he realized Eva wasn't right behind him. He walked over to sniff the floor where his bed had been and barked once, sharp and expectant..

Awakened by the noise, Reuben sauntered into the kitchen, a scowl on his face. *What's all the racket? I was trying to nap in case anyone is interested.* Before Eva could reply, Reuben noticed the empty spot in the corner usually occupied by Ginger's dog bed. *Does this mean the beast is finally leaving?*

Eva rolled her eyes when she saw his elated expression.

"Yes, Reuben. I just got a call from Maggie. We're leaving now and I may be gone for a while. I want to visit with her if she's up for it." She was about to get her coat and purse when she remembered the soup she'd made for Maggie that was in the fridge. "All right. Now we can go," she said placing the container in her quilted bag.

Take your time. I'm going to enjoy the peace and quiet.

Ginger walked over to Reuben and licked his face before Reuben had a chance to retreat.

Get away from me! I don't need your dog germs! Reuben hissed at him and ran into the living room.

Eva held her belly as she laughed. "Ginger, I haven't seen him move that fast in years." She wiped a tear from the corner of her eye with the back of her hand. "Okay. Let's go."

Ginger was already at the door, pawing at the handle and barking. *Hurry up. I can't wait!*

———

Maggie had been peeking out the window for the last five minutes, but her heart skipped a beat when Eva's car finally pulled into the driveway and she spotted Ginger. His nose was pressed against the rear passenger window and his front paws rested against the window frame.

Eva knew better than to make him wait while she retrieved his things from the trunk. He exploded out as though shot from a cannon when Eva swung the door open and he bolted toward the house. Maggie had already opened the door for them and was nearly bowled over.

Ginger continued to jump up and placed his paws on her thighs as he whined and then barked to greet her. Maggie knelt down and hugged him close, laughing even as tears rolled down her cheeks while Ginger licked her face non-stop.

Eva took the opportunity to get Ginger's things and the container of soup, then waited while they had their reunion. It took a moment before Maggie was able to extract herself.

"Be a good boy, Ginger, and let Eva come in," she told him and waved to invite Eva in. "Just put that down in the hall for now. I need a hug."

The women stood with their arms tightly around each other, too emotional to speak. At last, Eva broke the mood by patting her hand on Maggie's back. "Maggie, you're choking me."

Maggie quickly released her and backed away, embarrassed. "I'm so sorry."

Eva chuckled. "Don't apologize. I'm surprised I wasn't choking you, too. It's so good to see you," she said, clasping Maggie's hands in hers.

"You, too. Let's get this put away and catch up. The detectives told me you and your friends played a big part in finding me. I want to hear all about it."

They spent the next hour telling each other the events from Maggie's abduction to her rescue and Maggie's account of the trial. Ginger lay beside her with his head on Maggie's lap, not moving or allowing her to move while the women spoke.

"I'm so incredibly grateful to all of you. Would it be possible to thank all of you in person?" Maggie asked.

Eva smiled a Cheshire cat smile. "Now that you mention it. We'd like to have a homecoming party for you next week. It will be just the four of us and our partners and you. And of course, Ginger is invited too."

"I'd love that."

"Now that that's settled, I'll let you rest. I brought you a container of chicken soup with dumplings. I thought you might not be up to cooking today, but I didn't want you to go hungry."

"Thank you. You're the best, Eva."

"None of that," Eva warned when she saw Maggie's eyes watering. "You'll have me crying, too, and I need to see to drive home."

Maggie blinked and pursed her lips to hold back the tears, then smiled. She pushed up to say goodbye, but Ginger refused to move.

"Don't get up," Eva said, waving her down. "I can see myself out."

Once they were alone, Maggie stroked Ginger's head, still in her lap. At last, she felt a genuine sense of peace flow through her.

"I'm really, really home," she whispered.

CHAPTER 38

"That must be Maggie and Ginger," Eva announced when the doorbell rang.

They were the last to arrive and Eva was finally able to relax. She'd become nervous that meeting so many people might have been too much for Maggie so soon after her ordeal.

"Sorry, I'm late. I couldn't find Ginger's leash," Maggie explained as she shrugged off her jacket. Ginger waited at her side, still not ready to be far away from Maggie's touch.

"No need to apologize. I'm just glad you're here. We're all in the dining room and kitchen. You know how it is. No matter how big someone's house is, it seems like everyone always congregates where the food is."

Maggie had butterflies in her stomach—it was the kind of nervousness she'd pretended for years she never felt—when she saw all eyes turn to her and held Ginger's leash a little tighter for support. Eva steered Maggie by her elbow to the closest members of the group and Maggie relaxed a little when she recognized their faces.

"You've met Annalise and Jennifer, and you probably know David, too."

David greeted her with a smile. "If you ever need a dog-sitter, I bet Matthew and Nicole would be happy to help you out. And our Jack Russell, Boscoe, would probably enjoy a play date."

"I'll definitely keep that in mind."

"Let me introduce you to the others."

Their friendly greetings and genuine warmth eased any concerns Maggie had about fitting in, encouraging her to address them. "I want to thank all of you for your part in rescuing me. It may sound a little woo woo, but I really believe that I could feel your support. Knowing that I had people who would be looking for me, helped me get through each day and not give up hope. Never in my wildest dreams could I have imagined how so many people who didn't even know me would be a part of that."

"With these four women on your side, there wasn't any way that wouldn't happen," Jim told her. "I'm still amazed at the miracles they've pulled off in the time I've been privileged to know them."

Annalise looked up to see Liam gazing at her with new appreciation.

"I've always known you're special," Ashley whispered in Sarah's ear, making her blush. She wrapped her arm around Sarah's waist, grounding her. Sarah leaned in just a fraction—barely perceptible unless one knew her well.

"Enough of the mushy stuff, there's food and drinks, so grab yourselves a plate," Eva said to lighten the mood.

"You made my favorite—white chocolate raspberry cheese-cake!" Maggie exclaimed in delight when she spotted it among the assorted desserts and threw Eva an appreciative glance.

"You're welcome," Eva replied simply, giving her a wink.

Maggie made a point of speaking to each of the ladies individually and learned new information about their help—except for the paranormal skills they'd used. She was still unaware even of Eva's abilities.

Laughter and conversation filled the house and at one point

Eva caught Reuben glaring at her across the room, but she pretended not to hear when he said, *would you try to keep the noise down?*

The evening passed quickly until Eva interrupted them to make an announcement.

"Would everyone please gather in the living room?" She took Maggie's arm and led her to the center of the room. "We have something for you."

Maggie gave her a curious look, but followed with Ginger brushing against her leg as they walked.

Eva picked up a bundle from where she'd stashed it earlier to be out of sight, but handy for the presentation of the quilt.

"We'd already chosen Friendship Star as our pattern of the month because of the friendship the four of us have formed over the past year. But not long before you were taken, I read an article that brought the history and symbolism of the pattern home in a way I couldn't have imagined. I knew that the quilt was meant for you. Each of us has had a part in making it."

Eva handed the quilt to Maggie.

"I printed the article for you so you can read it later."

Maggie was overwhelmed by the gesture and had to gather her thoughts before speaking.

"Just when I thought coming home was the best part about this whole ordeal... you went and proved me wrong." She laughed low in her throat. "You'd think a reporter would know exactly what to say, but I'll never have the words to properly thank you all for what you've done."

"Open it so you can get the full effect," Eva encouraged. Jennifer and Sarah stepped up to hold the top edges so Maggie could step back to admire the quilt.

"Oh, look! Those are paw prints aren't they?" Maggie asked, delighted.

"Yes. I added those," Jennifer said, suddenly shy. "I thought Ginger should be a part of the project. In my mind, it represented him watching over you."

Maggie looked up from inspecting the quilt and met Jennifer's eyes. "I'll always think of that when I look at the quilt. Thank you."

She took the quilt back and folded it carefully, brushing her fingers over the fabric. "I will treasure this always." She paused. "I have a lot of associates, but I have only a few friends. I hope I can consider you all part of that group."

"We wouldn't have it any other way," Eva said. "Come on in, ladies. Group hug!"

After they'd broken apart, Jim stood next to Eva and clinked his glass to get the room's attention. He placed his hand at the small of Eva's back—subtle, steady, like he always did when he sensed she'd been carrying too much on her shoulders.

"Everyone grab their glasses. I'd like to make a toast." He waited until everyone had gathered around, their glasses in hand. "To Maggie—and to friendship. It's the gift that binds us together."

Glasses clinked as cheers of "Hear! Hear!" resounded.

Eva looked over at Reuben, sitting atop his cushion in the bay window and noticed Ginger had finally left Maggie's side. He hesitated and looked back at Maggie, then ambled toward the window—and Reuben. Her jaw dropped when he walked up to Reuben and placed his nose on the cat's and Reuben not only allowed it, but appeared to be reciprocating the gesture.

"To friendship, indeed," she whispered and raised her glass to them.

———

Continue the Series
The story isn't over yet.
Return to Glen Lake and see what the quilt club uncovers next.
Explore the Cozy Quilts Club Mysteries

———

Stay Connected
Join my reader newsletter
Be the first to hear about new releases, special discounts, and exclusive bonus content.
Sign up for the Newsletter at marshadefilippo.com
OR
Get notified automatically when new books release.
Follow me on Amazon
Follow me on BookBub

————

A Quick Favor
Reviews help other readers discover the Cozy Quilts Club mysteries.

If you enjoyed this book, would you consider leaving a short review on Amazon? Even a few sentences make a difference.

Thank you for being part of the quilt circle.

ALSO BY MARSHA DEFILIPPO

Arizona Dreams (The Arizona Series)

Later-in-life romances about second chances, lasting love, and deep emotional connection—with on-page intimacy.

Arizona Dreams (Seasons of the Heart)

Later-in-life romances about second chances and lasting love—told in a clean, closed-door style.

The Destiny Inn series

A gentle magical-realism series set in a timeless inn, where travelers arrive when they need it most and leave forever changed.

A Cozy Quilts Club Mystery series

A cozy mystery series featuring a small-town quilt club whose members use their paranormal gifts to solve murders—one stitch at a time.

The Quilt of Forgotten Secrets

A Cozy Quilts Club Bonus Story. Available as Ebook and Audiobook formats

Read: https://BookHip.com/MCXWBJK

Listen: https://ihave.spoken.press/p/6f6i3VshmzU

ABOUT THE AUTHOR

After retiring from her day job of nearly 33 years, Marsha DeFilippo has embarked on a new career of writing books. She is also a quilter and lifelong avid crafter who has yet to try a craft she doesn't like. She spends her winters in Arizona and the remainder of the year in Maine.

For more information, please visit my website:
marsha defilippo.com

To get the latest information on new releases, excerpts and more, be sure to sign up for Marsha's newsletter.
https://marshadefilippo.com/newsletter

f facebook.com/Marsha-DeFilippo
instagram.com/marshadefilippo
BB bookbub.com/authors/marsha-defilippo
pinterest.com/defilippo0699
a amazon.com/author/marshadefilippo
marshadefilippowriter.substack.com

Made in the USA
Monee, IL
07 July 2026

56544772R00100